The Makeweight

First published in 2023 by Ely's Arch
an imprint of Liberties Press
Dublin, Ireland
libertiespress.com

Distributed in the UK by
Casemate UK
casematepublishing.co.uk

Distributed in the United States and Canada by
Casemate IPM
casematepublishers.com

2 4 6 8 10 9 7 5 3 1
A CIP record for this title is available from the British Library.
Cover design by Baker @ Plan B Associates

The Makeweight

Philip Davison

Jack Hinkley's story stops short of the momentous changes that began in Europe of 1989. The role he fulfilled does not. As a result of these changes there has been some diversification, that is all. The makeweight will always be needed.

Part One

1

Our Man had been watching the three hijackers closely. Bunglers, he thought. The leader, the one with the tic, was smart, but you had to be smart all the time if you weren't going to bungle a hijacking. He had given the grenade to the youngster. That was a mistake.

Our Man had taken note of the pair of knitting needles a passenger in an adjacent seat had in the bag at her feet. He had decided that the hijacker holding the middle portion of the plan, the quiet one with the machine-gun, was the most dangerous one. He was alert and relatively calm. A knitting needle through his temple would greatly improve the odds of getting out alive if shooting were to begin.

The one with the tic began to administer a vicious beating with the butt of his pistol. He had chosen to punish a young American. Wailing from several passengers made him more violent. Our Man watched attentively. He screwed up his eyes, but couldn't quite make out whether or not the safety catch on the pistol was engaged.

At Lord's cricket ground, tactically, it was time for tea. England were being routed. A telephone on a long cord was brought to the gent standing at a window making little noises of disgust.

'For you, sir.'

'Thank you.' The gent, known to some as C, waited for the bringer of the telephone to withdraw before taking the call. 'Yes?'

There was a concise briefing from the other end. When it was complete C issued his instruction in a flat voice. 'Kill them.'

When he put down the receiver he called to the chairman of the club. 'George,' he said, 'isn't it time for tea?'

'Five minutes more, wouldn't you say?' came the reply.

C made more of his sea-noises.

The hijacked jet was now landing to refuel at Bercelona Airport. Action was taken immediately, on the presumption that the hijackers would be expecting lengthy negotiations to exchange a few passengers for fuel. There had been some sort of coded communication between the tower and the captain after he had pressed the HIJACK button. He taxied the jet more or less into the right position on the tarmac in front of the main terminal building, but the hijacker with the tic sliced off the navigator's ear with a knife. This was punishment for the pilot's hesitancy in obeying his order to taxi the jet to a position on the airport apron.

Even before the navigator's ear came away, the assault on the aircraft had begun.

In the event, the three hijackers were killed. Four passengers died of wounds sustained from a grenade-blast. Others were injured.

Jack Hinkley, MI6 Station Head in Barcelona, was at once appalled and relieved. In this respect his reaction was no different than most others'. However, for him, there was a most unexpected twist to this act of air-piracy. It rekindled in him a belief that fate eventually ensured the redress of all imbalance. Somehow, man had become blind to this process, having lost the ability to read the signs in the pattern of birds in flight, having lost the animal's receptiveness to that which is borne in the air. That kind of thinking was a luxury, of course. Somewhere else, some poor bastard with a job not unlike his was being asked how he had let three armed terrorists board a plane.

Earlier that day he had been thinking about the grass growing in England. He was thinking about swimming in the Lido in Hyde Park. For an underworked Jack Hinkley, it was threatening to be another sultry day spent in Barcelona, a city in which he felt comfortable only at night. The moderating sea breeze so often referred to in the tourist guides was again absent. His small office – an apartment located on the Paslo de Colon, a busy waterfront street with heavy façades – was once again a heat-box. The office plants were ailing. Their soil was choking from cigarette-ash. They had been watered too often with tepid tea. The air-conditioning had been on full tilt all day, and when it was working flat out it made a racket. It had given Hinkley a headache. He was tired of watching the cable-car ply between the harbour and Montjuïc, or rather, that part of each journey he could observe from the window. When news of the hijacking first came in, he had been sitting around waiting for a message, a one-way call. It was almost six o'clock. He was anxious to go home. He wanted to have a shower, drink some iced tea, have a late siesta. Then he might feed the cat – if it showed up, that is. It wasn't a likeable cat. After that he had planned to go out walking. He might stop for a drink in a bar he frequented near the bird market. Then he would visit Pilar. He would bring her fresh bread and cheese for tomorrow's breakfast. She would ignore this gesture. She would swagger about her pokey apartment in her bare feet, haranguing him in thick Catalan. He would offer a comprehensive apology for having been drunk and morose the previous week.

When news of the hijacking came in, Davis was standing in for the new man, Higgins. Higgins was meant to be on night-duty, but was suffering from vicious stomach-cramps. Larch, in ciphers, was the only other person present. The station was advised that the British Airways jet would be landing at Barcelona Airport to refuel, before continuing to Beirut.

While Hinkley and, presumably, every other intelligence officer in the city was assessing the information available, diplomatic pressure was being brought to bear on the Spanish authorities. The British Consul General had already contacted the Spanish Foreign Ministry in an attempt to ascertain what the authorities' response would be to the hijackers' demand to be allowed to refuel at Barcelona. No immediate answer was forthcoming.

The jet had a full complement, the majority of the passengers being Britons and Germans. The identity of the hijackers was now known. Photographs and profiles were forwarded to Barcelona Station together with the passenger list and other flight details.

The consensus in those capitals immediately affected was that under no circumstances was the jet to be allowed to refuel and continue to Beruit. However, the politicians and diplomats were not moving fast enough. A decision had already been taken at Lord's cricket ground.

The media reacted swiftly, but not as swiftly as the anti-terrorist squad. One local television crew did manage to catch the assault on the jet in shakey telephoto shots. It looked like a badly directed action sequence of a film in which the special effects failed to live up to expectation.

Hinkley, Davis and Larch watched the bizarre scene on the office television. All they could do was answer the telephone and make their report. So they thought. Then came the twist. The television cameras caught the survivors descending the steps from the forward door of the jet. Among the passengers observed disembarking was Our Man, known to Hinkley as Major Klinovec. Klinovec was Deputy Head of Directorate S of the First Chief Directorate of the KGB. His department controlled Soviet agents in the field. Hinkley was, as far as he knew, the only British intelligence officer to have met Klinovec, albeit briefly. Now, inspite of the distraction of an over-zealous on-the-spot television reporter frequently filling much of the frame, he was sure he had seen Klinovec among the survivors.

Hinkley recalled tendering his report on his encounter with Major Klinovec. C had summoned him to his office. The old man had stared out his window for a long time before turning to study him intently through smudged glasses. He had leaned against his desk and had gravely tapped the thin file with a rheumatic finger, but had said nothing about its content. 'You've done well,' he had mumbled as an afterthought. Though nothing was said, he knew his boss had made allowances for his inexperience.

Shortly after that meeting Hinkley was transferred from Berlin to the Iberian Desk in London. There, he worked hard to impress his superiors. He showed himself to be adept with files. He produced reliable analysis. Subsequently, there had been a number of confused reports from Barcelona.

C appointed Hinkley head of that small station. Now, Hinkley was sure that it would be on his handling of this crisis that he would finally be judged.

He had to think fast. Klinovec was a shrewd man obsessed with security. He was not often in Moscow, but when he was he stayed at a modest address on Prospekt Mira. That was the only address for him known to Western intelligence. Out of Moscow, he never slept in the same bed on any two consecutive nights. If, as in this instance, there was additional cause for concern, undoubtedly he would go to ground and draw on his considerable resources to organise his safe passage out of danger.

A flash signal was sent to London seeking specific instructions, but a quick response would not be quick enough in this instance. Hinkley was forced to act immediately. 'We're going to meet him,' he announced.

By 'meet him' the crew knew he meant 'snatch him'. Why snatch him? For hard information that might come from interrogation. To cast doubt. To nurture suspicion among his masters and peers in Moscow Centre. Circumstantial evidence of treachery could by fabricated over time. Furthermore, there was the remote possibility that he might actually be turned.

'What about London?' Larch asked, attempting to hide his concern.

'There isn't time. Was he alone?'

'I think so,' said Davis, 'but we didn't see all the passengers getting off.'

Hinkley tossed the print-out of the passenger list on his desk. 'This isn't going to tell us. We'll assume he was travelling alone.' He issued Larch with a message for London. He instructed him to telephone Higgins, to get him out of his sick-bed, to tell him Hinkley was on his way to collect him. Davis was to take up a position outside the building known to be used by the KGB. Hinkley and Higgins would go to the airport, then on to the hotel, or whatever the authorities were using as a rest-centre for the survivors.

'Larch,' he concluded, 'when you're finished that, I want you to watch Snitkina's apartment. He just might go there.'

Snitkina was attached to the Soviet diplomatic corps. He was, in fact, from Line KR, a branch of the KGB responsible for penetrating foreign intelligence, and for keeping their house in order abroad. He had been sent to Barcelona to reorganise the station. Like so many KGB stations, it was overstaffed. Too many officers had come from the Second Chief Directorate, from the provinces where they had been skilled in internal repression. They lacked linguistic skills and in general had a poorer education than their colleagues in Moscow. Moscow Centre had embarked upon a purge within its ranks. Snitkina and his team were weeding world-wide. Hinkley had a fat file on him. Snitkina was the principal investigator in what the Soviets designated the Fifth Geographic Department: France, Italy, Spain, Belgium, Holland, Luxembourg and Ireland. Snitkina had started in Line N, an outfit that collected data and recruited low-level agents. After serving in the Czech intelligence service, the bright young Klinovec had been recruited into the same Line N. He had held a junior post while Snitkina was still in that office. It was possible that Klinovec knew of Snitkina's presence in Barcelona, that he would avoid the local goons and call on a name from the past.

The office would have to be left unattended once the call had been put through to London. The operation needed eight to ten people. As it was, Hinkley would have to make do with four. There was no one else available that evening.

They took long-range walkie-talkies. Davis went directly to the KGB building and sat in his car across the street from the main entrance. He also had a view of the mouth of the narrow lane that served a side entrance and garage. Larch drove most of the way to Snitkina's apartment. He parked two streets away and walked the remaining distance. The apartment was on a quiet street. A man sitting in a car would be conspicuous. There was no café in which to sit. No real cover from which to watch. He had no option but to patrol. He was nervous. He felt sure he would be outsmarted in the dirty-tricks department. This wasn't a radio operator's game.

2

Hinkley drove to Higgins's apartment at a dangerous speed. He, too, was afraid of being outwitted, outmanoeuvred, or simply outrun. He had a box in his pocket with a syringe in it, a stiff tranquilliser in its barrel. Would he get close enough to inject Klinovec? It was against procedure, but London would have to understand.

Pale-faced and sweaty, Higgins shambled into the car. Hinkley briefed him on the way to the airport. Higgins had the station gun and looked like he might use it on himself. 'Christ,' he said, winding down the window, 'I'm going to throw up.'

'Do it,' snapped Hinkley unsympathetically, and made a point of watching. Higgins vomited to order.

Security was heavy at the airport. Hinkley and Higgins showed diplomatic passports and were directed to a hotel in sight of the airport. The foyer was crowded with displaced guests. The survivors had been split up. Some had been taken to hospital with serious injuries, together with others suffering from shock, concussion, lacerations. Klinovec had come down the steps from the jet unscathed. Hinkley and Higgins moved watchfully among the confused crowd. Higgins was as sick now as he had been when he had vomited

11

from the car window. They couldn't ask for Klinovec. They didn't know the name under which he had chosen to travel. They had no photograph of Klinovec to show. They couldn't be sure he was travelling alone.

Hinkley asked an airline official if all passengers had been accounted for. It was difficult to say, came the candid reply. They had not yet been able to collect all the passports. The passengers had been dispersed too soon. They were still checking against the flight list. The distress among the passengers was considerable.

Hinkley again presented his British consulate credentials and asked to see those passports that had been collected.

He would have to wait. The passports were not immediately available.

Already, it was turning into a nightmare. The horrific event had produced chaos. Even an amateur could slip away unnoticed. Perhaps – just perhaps – Klinovec thought he was safe, that his anonymity was protected in the aftermath of the bloody attack. Survivors would be shielded; they would be hurried to their destinations. Perhaps he thought it was safer to stay.

About eight kilometres north of the airport, in the city, Davis was sitting low in the driver's seat. Nothing was happening. He was fidgety, but only because in the rush to get to the job he had left his cigarettes in the office. Of the four, he was the best field operator, though Hinkley had the brains. Higgins had had some field experience but wanted a desk-job in London. He wasn't at all pleased with his new post in Barcelona. Davis was quite the opposite. He didn't mind the heat. He knew where to eat, too. Like Hinkley,

Davis was patient. If Klinovec showed up, Davis was sure he could keep track of him. In the meantime, he'd just have to wait for a smoke. He had already smoked the cigarette he kept in the sun-visor.

Still farther north, near the Parque de la Ciudadela, Larch saw a lone figure approaching on foot. Larch was patrolling on the same side of the street as him. They were walking towards each other. Larch had just passed Snitkina's apartment. He made the mistake of crossing the street. He should have walked right past him. He had made his positive identification, but he had drawn attention to himself.

At the airport hotel Hinkley and Higgins were busy hunting among the survivors. They didn't hear Larch's call. Higgins had left the walkie-talkie in the car.

Davis heard Larch's call. He responded quickly. He was not more than two kilometres away, but when he got to Snitkina's apartment he could not find Larch. He drove around the block twice. No sign of Larch. The street was quiet, as it usually was. A Mercedes was parked in front of Snitkina's apartment building. Davis recognised it on his first run down the street.

There were three KGB goons in it: two in the front, one in the back. On Davis's second pass the one in the driver's seat raised a small bottle shrouded in brown paper, a sort of salute to Davis.

Davis didn't make a third pass. He stopped the car in the adjacent street and tried to make contact with Hinkley. The airport was still within range for the radio. Why was there no response? Davis wasn't feeling so smart now. He had been watching an empty office while its workers were out on business. Now here they were, the smug bastards, business done.

At this point, Hinkley was convinced that Klinovic had not come to the hotel. Higgins offered no option on the matter. They completed their check on the rooms. Higgins vomited again, this time in the foyer. The vomiting didn't bother Hinkley. It was Higgins leaving the walkie-talkie in the car that made him furious. The police weren't surprised to see the diplomat throw up. It was just another weak-stomached foreigner letting go. Hinkley advised the senior police officer on duty to expect another party from the British consulate. They would facilitate the swift and safe passage of the British contingent to Paris, the intended destination of the British Airways flight. He was, of course, anticipating the arrival of the legitimate consulate staff. The American team had already arrived.

As it happened, Hinkley and Higgins encountered two British consulate officials in the car park.

'Jack,' one called.

Hinkley ignored them. Higgins followed suit. The officials didn't like being ignored, but they didn't hang about. They went into the hotel, one tightening his tie, the other buttoning his jacket.

Hinkley got through to Davis on the walkie-talkie. The worst-case scenario had come to pass. They had been out-manoeuvred, and now Larch was missing. They had no way of knowing whether the KGB outside Snitkina's apartment was a decoy or a bodyguard. Of Hinkley, Higgins and Davis, none had seen Klinovic or, for that matter, Snitkina. They could only assume that Larch was, or had been, in hot pursuit; that either they had picked him up, or his walkie-talkie was faulty. Hinkley instructed Davis to wait where he was until he and Higgins arrived, or Klinovec broke cover.

They travelled the eight or nine kilometres from Prat de Llobregat to Snitkina's apartment as quickly as they had covered the ground to the airport. The airport road was a favourite stretch for speed-traps, but that evening it was clear. They rendezvoused with Davis. They parked up the street from the Mercedes. London would be shouting by now. Signals would be printing out in the empty Barcelona office.

Hinkley was sure they had lost Klinovec. Davis said Klinovec might still be in Snitkina's apartment. They would wait. If he had already left the building, Larch would be on his tail. He would make contact when he could.

For ten minutes they watched and waited in silence. Nothing happened. Then the garage door lifted, a car emerged and broke from the lane at speed. There was just a driver visible.

'He's on the floor,' said Hinkley.

'No he's not,' retorted Davis.

Hinkley turned the key in the ignition.

'That's what they want us to think,' insisted Davis. 'He's driving too fast.'

'You can't be sure.'

'I fucking am. He's either going with *them*' – he indicated the Mercedes – 'or he's already left.'

'Christ.'

The car was soon out of sight. Hinkley kept his motor running.

'Larch was sure he saw him?'

'All he said was "I think I've got him. It's him." Then seconds later, "He's gone into the building." Larch wanted us here fast. He was pissing himself.'

'Klinovec won't travel with a big escort. He won't get in that car. He won't mark himself like that. If there's an escort they'll keep their distance.'

'If they *were* going with him they'd have come out of there like elephants, one after another,' said Davis. 'He'd be last – like he's part of the escort. That's what they do. I don't think he's in there. I think he's long gone.'

'Back to the airport?'

'No. Bus or train. Preferably train, but he won't be fussy. He'll take whatever is going out first. He'll re-route once, maybe twice . . . if he hasn't cancelled. Personally, I think he'll cancel. He'll go and see a shoemaker who'll give him a new identity, then he'll go home.'

'I agree,' said Hinkley reluctantly. He ordered Higgins to stay in Davis's car and watch the apartment while he and Davis went to the railway station. They were now desperate. The decision to go to the railway station was nothing more than an informed guess. Neither man believed they would catch up with him.

At the railway station they virtually bumped into Klinovec. Had it been Hinkley by himself Klinovic would have easily evaded him. But he had Davis. Davis was a cold fish. Strong, too. He caught Klinovec by the throat. He gave a snorty, familiar laugh, as if he was play-acting.

'Not many people die standing up, did you know that?' When Davis spoke, the bully in him surfaced. Even Hinkley was shocked at the speed and power with which the grip had been applied. Bystanders didn't see what was really happening. They didn't see the skin change colour.

Hinkley kept one hand in his pocket as though he was carrying a gun. Davis was carrying a pistol, but drew no attention to it. Klinovec had been taken by surprise, but he knew what was happening to him. He realised that for the moment, it was pointless to resist.

Suddenly, Davis let go. Klinovec caught his breath with difficulty. For all his ruthlessness, Klinovec seemed a weak man physically. The choking had damaged him. He was shaken. Davis glared at him – a glare that said, *I can cripple you, I can kill*. Klinovec knew better than to run.

'What do you want from me?' he asked in an uneven voice.

Davis moaned wearily. 'Let's go,' he said, pointing towards the main station exit with his chin.

They started to walk, Davis behind Klinovec, Hinkley falling in beside him.

'We've met before,' said Hinkley. 'Berlin.'

If Klinovec did recognise him, he was not acknowledging it. Hinkley's heart was pounding.

'You remember?'

'No.'

'Klinovec was perspiring. Not from fear. From heat. Like Higgins, he belonged in a cool, temperate climate. He had no overcoat, but he was ill-dressed for the heat. He wore a tweed jacket, a pullover, a long-sleeved shirt, heavy trousers. Evidently he had been well advised as to the weather in Paris.

In the car Klinovec asked not *where* he was being taken, but rather *to whom*. He wouldn't take off his jacket.

He knew what was coming. He said a drug wasn't necessary, that a blindfold would do, but Hinkley wanted him in a stupor. It had to be done fast. They had parked away from the traffic, but their privacy was not guaranteed. Klinovec wasn't going to sit still for the injection. The primed syringe struck fear into him. Rather than fight over the jacket, Davis held him while Hinkley sunk the needle through the cloth of his trousers, which clung to his thighs with sweat. He pushed home the plunger. He had, as Davis was quick to point out, produced the syringe too soon, and now he was too slow in removing the needle from the muscle. The victim fought. The needle snapped off the syringe, but the dose had been administered. It took effect rapidly. Davis was soon able to push him into a heap in the corner of the back seat. Hinkley sat back in the driver's seat and started the engine. Davis picked at the broken needle in Klinovec's leg.

'Can you get it?' Hinkley asked, glancing in the rear-view mirror.

'Need his trousers off,' replied Davis, sitting back in his seat. *He* seemed able to relax. 'Might need a tweezers, too. Have you got a cigarette, Jack? I've smoked my last.'

Hinkley made contact with Higgins on the walkie-talkie. There had been no movement at Snitkina's apartment. The Mercedes was still conspicuously parked outside the building, its occupants drinking inconspicuously. There was no sign of Larch.

Hinkley needed to contact London urgently. Now that he had his man, he needed instructions. Klinovec would soon be missed. He'd have to get him out of Barcelona fast. He didn't care how much dope they'd have to pump into him. There would be plenty of time for his head to clear. It would be a long interrogation. Hinkley had decided to take him to a yacht anchored in the harbour. The yacht belonged to his Spanish friend Xavier. He stopped the car outside a busy street café. In the back seat Davis linked arms with his charge. They didn't want him slumping forward. He was more concerned about being illegally parked than he was about the possible arrival of the Komitet Gosudarstvennoy Bezopasnosti.

Hinkley called Xavier from the café telephone. 'I need to borrow your yacht, Xavier. Tonight.'

Xavier, a wealthy shoe manufacturer, had befriended Jack Hinkley when Hinkley was screening those bordellos in Barcelona frequented by Eastern Bloc diplomats and KGB for potential bed-spies. Xavier, forever in search of what he saw as sophisticated comradeship, knew Hinkley worked at the British consulate. They had been formally introduced at a party. He saw Jack as some sort of trouble-shooter who prevented the blackmailing of British businessmen and diplomats by the use of sophisticated threats. They had become close friends. Xavier used to introduce Jack to his friends as a British spy.

Davis waited in the car with Sleeping Beauty at the bottom of the drive while Hinkley called to collect the keys. Hinkley told his friend he wanted to impress a woman. Xavier liked Hinkley's directness, the soft Englishness of it.

'There are two bottles of Champagne in the fridge,' he advised as his wife came to the door to greet Hinkley. Hinkley kissed the woman on the cheek.

'Bring your friend here to dinner,' she said, smiling.

Hinkley kissed her again, on the other cheek.

19

★

It was early for Miguel, the boatman, to be drunk, but he recognised Hinkley, his employer's friend. He was happy to surrender the launch and cover the short distance to the bar with his jittery shoogle of a walk.

Putting Klinovec in the launch was easy by comparison to getting him out and onto the yacht. Had it not been for Davis's exceptionally strong arms pulling from the yacht deck, their captive would have been lost in the gentle swell.

So far as they could tell, the abduction had gone unobserved by the KGB. Klinovec had insisted on moving without an escort, it would appear. The only movement at Snitkina's apartment was Higgins opening his car door to vomit. His stomach had nothing left to heave up. He was quite dizzy. He would have given a lot to have been able to lie flat on the cold concrete pavement.

While Davis baby-sat on the yacht, Hinkley returned to land, and drove the car to the office. The building was quiet. Very quiet. There was nothing unusual about that. It was Friday night. Offices were closed. Residents were out. Families were promenading on the Ramblas. He took the ancient lift to the floor above the office. He could see as he passed that his corridor was deserted. When he got out of the lift, he paused to listen. Nothing was stirring in the building. Cautiously, he descended the stairs to the floor below and entered the office. It was as they had left it, save for the additional coded print-out.

Hinkley was jumpy. The innocence of the place disturbed him. Larch's disappearance made the whole set-up unsafe. Hinkley was intent on leaving nothing to chance. He took the print-out and, with difficulty, decoded it in the car as he drove slowly. The orders from London were clear: to maintain surveillance, to keep Paris informed, to report to London. A second message had a greater sense of urgency about it. It gave a number – not one of the firm's numbers known to Hinkley – and the name 'Dovecot', to be contacted immediately. The name was familiar. It was a pen-name C used.

He made his call from a public telephone.

'Farrington here. I want to speak to Mr Dovecot.'

'One moment, please.'

There was a pause, then the voice asked: 'Are we on an open line?'

'Yes.'

'Your number, please.'

Hinkley read off the telephone number listed in the kiosk.

'Have you been compromised?' asked the voice.

'Possibly.'

'Ring again in fifteen minutes.'

The line went dead.

It was a long fifteen minutes. Hinkley thought about the hole in Klinovec's sock revealed by the loss of a shoe as they struggled with him between launch and yacht. He had a hole in his sock. What would London do with this six-cylinder agent with a hole in his sock, Hinkley wondered. How would they play him?

'Farringdon here. I want to speak to Mr Dovecot.'

'Mr Dovecot is not available. Call Mr Jeffers.'

The line went dead.

Hinkley's worries had caused him to send an emergency alarm signal. He had in that brief exchange on the telephone declared that he believed the Barcelona office to be bugged. Now he would have to call Jeffers in Madrid. Jeffers would carry London's message. He would have to use his one-time pad, a tiny booklet with letter code based on random groups of five letters designed to be used just once between two parties. Hinkley kept his pad rolled in the tag of one of his shoelaces. The one identical pad was held by Special Dispatch in London.

Hinkley rang Jeffers.

'Yes?'

'Farrington here. You have a message for me.'

The letter groups were read to him. Decoded, the message had two instructions: to free Klinovec immediately; to fly to London immediately thereafter.

Hinkley was dumbfounded.

Davis had a bottle of Champagne out. It was on the cabin table together with two glasses and his pistol. Klinovec, huddled in the corner, was coming to his senses. Hinkley called Davis up on deck.

'He's coming round,' said Davis. 'Shall I give him another shot?'

'No.'

'Another degenerate,' said Davis contemptuously. 'Another Quiet One.' 'Quiet One' was the term used by Moscow Centre for a homosexual. 'And don't look at me like that. I haven't been playing with him. I can fucking tell, that's all.'

22

'What size shoes do you wear?' snapped Hinkley.

'Nines. Why?'

'Mine are eights. He's got big feet. Give him yours.'

'What?' said Davis indignantly.

'I said: give him your shoes,' ordered Hinkley. 'We're moving him now.'

'What's happened?'

'Do it!' shouted Hinkley.

Davis reluctantly did as he was told. He soon emerged from the cabin, holding the odd shoe.

'I suppose I get this?'

'Get him up here.'

'He's had the labels removed,' said Davis, looking inside the shoe, but you can tell it's East German crap.' He tossed the shoe overboard.

When Davis emerged from the cabin with his dopey charge, he had removed his socks as well as shoes, so as not to slip on the varnished deck. He was no less malevolent-appearing in his bare feet.

'Where are we taking him?' he asked out of earshot of the subject, who stood trying to focus on the harbour lights.

'We're letting him go,' replied Hinkley blankly.

'What?'

'You heard me. Get him in the launch.'

In the launch, Klinovec remained silent. He seemed to know he was safe. Davis knew not to ask questions. Hinkley was doing some deep thinking.

They drove Klinovec to the railway station. There was still time for him to catch a late train. In the car he had his trousers opened, his hand inside one leg. Extracting the broken piece of needle from his thigh was proving difficult and painful. He was still disorientated. Davis sat in the back seat, staring at him brutishly. When he got tired of watching him, he gazed glumly out of the window at the pedestrians, dark against the lighted shop-fronts.

Hinkley could scarcely keep his eyes on the road. He kept glancing in the mirror at the silent, winsome figure beside Davis in the back seat.

'Thank you for the shoes,' said Klinovec, getting out of the car at the station. Clearly, Davis' shoes were at least one size too small on the man's feet.

'Don't mention it,' replied Davis, who continued to look out of the window in the opposite direction.

Klinovec paused for a moment, as though he wanted to say something to Hinkley, or perhaps, to allow Hinkley to speak.

Hinkley said nothing.

Klinovec said nothing.

David had again turned to stare.

Klinovec shuffled unsteadily into the station.

'He's a bit like your pal, Miguel, on the docks,' said Davis disparagingly. 'Should have given him the other bottle of Champagne along with my shoes.'

Hinkley called Higgins on the walkie-talkie, told him to go home and nurse his stomach.

Davis picked at his feet in the back seat on their way to the office to wait for Larch to call.

There was still time to catch a late flight to London but Hinkley was concerned about Larch. He made two reservations: one for the last flight that night, the second for the first flight the following morning. That was as long as he dared delay.

They sat in the office with the fan whirring. The notepad on Hinkley's desk ruffled with each measured current of air on each sweep of the fan. It was one of those minor annoyances that provided a point of focus for one whose patience was being tried. They had searched in vain for a listening device. Now they sat in silence, waiting for Larch to call.

By 1 AM there had been no call.

'Will I try his apartment again?' asked Davis.

'Yes,' said Hinkley curtly. The whole business was getting to him. Yesterday, Klinovec had been his enemy, the man who, in Berlin, had conned him into betraying one of his fledgling agents, thereby sealing his doom. Today, Klinovec was his friend – a friendship that would be betrayed were it known that British agents had kidnapped him, then let him go.

Hinkley tried hard to think of another reason for the extraordinary instruction from London. Perhaps he was being deceived, but the order had come from C through Special Dispatch. There would be a record. It didn't make sense. The logical explanation was that Klinovec was working for London.

Once again, it seemed, Hinkley had been duped, and now, a man was missing. The Barcelona Station had been isolated. The unforgiveable had happened: Hinkley had lost control.

Davis rang Larch's apartment again.

'Peter Davis, Mrs Larch. I'm awfully sorry to be disturbing you again . . . Richard hasn't just stepped in the door by any chance? It is rather urgent, you see . . . .'

Davis's syrupy manner made Hinkley shift in his chair.

'Not to worry,' continued Davis. 'I expect he's still at the airport. This nasty business will keep us busy throughout the night . . . .'

Mrs Larch wasn't worried. Her husband was press secretary at the consulate. He'd have plenty to do that night.

'You will have to ring me as soon as he comes in, or indeed, if he phones you . . . you're so kind . . . why yes, that *would* be nice. Eight o'clock, Sunday evening. I shan't eat, in anticipation. Goodnight, Mrs Larch.'

Smarmy get, thought Hinkley. He'd just as happily eat the hard skin he had picked off his feet in the back of the car.

'Well?' said Davis, challenging the expression on Hinkley's face.

'Go home. I'll wait. Pick me up here at 6AM unless you hear otherwise.'

Davis let out a long, reproachful sigh. He held Hinkley responsible for what he saw as a botched operation. He wanted to say: you just couldn't wait, could you?

'Call to my place on your way home . . . in case he's waiting there for some reason.'

Another disapproving sigh, this one more from the stomach.

'Right.'

'And if he calls you . . . .'

'Right.'

Davis paused in the doorway.

'You owe me a pair of shoes.'

He was wearing the plimsolls he kept in the office for when he went jogging on the seafront. Davis was a fit fucker.

★

Hinkley sat by the telephone all night, dry-lipped, blinking, breathing unevenly. It was a familiar sensation shared by those who ran agents. There was no getting used to the waiting. The walkie-talkie lay on the desk, channel open. The fan whirred. The paper fluttered. From his chair he surveyed the office in search of listening devices. When he got tired of that, he pulled dead leaves off the plants. He watched the night traffic thin in the street below. He shaved with the battery razor he kept in his drawer. He scrubbed his teeth with a dry toothbrush. There was no call.

At 5 AM he called Higgins. He didn't ask how Higgins felt. He just ordered him to get over to the office by 6 AM.

'I'm all right now, thanks Jack,' said Higgins sourly.

Hinkley put down the receiver sharply. Higgins would have to go.

Higgins arrived just before Davis. He hadn't cleaned out Hinkley's car. It stank of vomit. He was left to wait for Larch's call. Davis drove Hinkley to his apartment in his car. The stink of stale tobacco was preferable to vomit.

Hinkley lived on the lower slope of Tabidabo in a fashionable district north of the medieval quarter, where most of the tourists congregated. His was a quiet street. There was a small café/tobacconist on one corner, a cluster of expensive outfitters adjacent. Like the office, the apartment was small, but it was comfortable. The firm had it on a long lease at favourable terms. The firm was admired by other services for, if nothing else, its record in acquiring information and premises on the cheap.

Davis sat in the car outside while Hinkley packed the smallest of a set of three suitcases his wife, Mary, had given him.

At the airport Hinkley was paged. It was Higgins calling. The consulate had been in touch. Larch's body had been found floating face down in the Rio Besos. The KGB probably had the body in the boot of the Mercedes when they saluted Davis with the bottle in the bag.

3

Klinovec would be safe in the East by now, thought Hinkley as the acceleration of the jet engines pressed him into his seat. How many lives had been lost or ruined to protect the man? The question, Hinkley knew, would never be answered. Strangely, the Klinovec revelation didn't seem to matter to Hinkley at that moment. He was grieving for Richard Larch, and for himself.

In the arrivals hall his daughter stood waving car keys in the air. In her car on the way to Chelsea, Hinkley had a compelling urge to tell her all about his devious, audacious and sorry life, but he held back. Vanessa did much of the talking.

'Are you tired? You must be . . . . Will you be staying long. I know you're secretly busy . . . . Mother will be so pleased you've come to stay, don't you think? . . . I expect she'll find it difficult to say so . . . .'

'How is she?' Hinkley asked.

'Well,' she replied in a lower voice. 'She might be late home. She had arranged to visit Father Green.'

'Father Green?'

'Sounds innocent, don't you think?' Vanessa added cheekily.

'Like Hayden's Toy Symphony.'

Now that her father had committed himself, she concluded harshly, 'Father Green's a dirty old bugger.'

There was a pause, then Vanessa spoke again.

'She's been waiting in for the men to come and fix the central heating.'

'What's wrong with the heating?'

'Oh, I don't know. Air bubbles, I expect. Anyway, they were finishing when I came upstairs to see if she was coming to the airport, but she was already late for her holy visit.'

The last part of the journey was spent in silence. Incongruously, Hinkley thought about telling his little girl stories from his childhood – his earliest encounter with specialists – with juju men: Wednesday afternoons in a Liverpool primary school, there'd be a visit to one of the local factories. Jam-makers, bakers, sausage manufacturers: they were the best. Bugger the factories that made cardboard boxes, furniture, rivets. You wanted something you could eat at the other end. You asked the man for his autograph, then waited for the goods.

Randomly, he thought about his mother and the cinema-owner. Thought about being given his free pass and sixpence for the matinee before the couple locked themselves in the manager's office for the duration of the performance.

Even as a child he had an eye for the details that betray secrets. He had told neither of them that what he had learnt as an adult was that no one secret was a whole truth.

Some time ago Hinkley had decided that there was, quite literally, no reason his wife should care to listen, for she too recognised that in all matters pertaining to the service, there could only be fidelity in silence. He clung silently to his secrecy, just as they to their respective titles: wife and daughter. There was security in his darkness. The nothingness of it had the power to preserve without favour both juju man and adulterer.

★

Hinkley carried his suitcase from the car. As he climbed the steps to the hall door, he noticed that the façade and railings of the house had been freshly painted. Every room, it seemed, was lit, including the basement, which Vanessa had turned into a self-contained flat for herself.

Hinkley rummaged for his key to the hall door.

'Mother's had the locks changed,' Vanessa said. 'You'll have to come through the basement.'

'Don't you have a key to the hall door?'

'No, just to my place . . . and I have a key to the door at the top of the basement stairs inside. Are you sure you don't want me to carry your case?'

'Quite sure.'

Vanessa led her father down the steps to the basement.

'Why did she change the locks?' Hinkley asked, peeved at not having a key to his own house.

'There have been a lot of robberies in the neighbourhood recently.'

'Did she have a London Bar and hinge-bolts fitted?'

'I expect so.'

'You don't know?'

'Well, I never looked.'

'What about the basement door? If they're going to break in, more than likely it will be through the basement door or window.'

Hinkley examined both. There was no London Bar, no hinge-bolts, no window-locks installed.

'I suppose I should have had it done long ago,' he mumbled.

They passed through the basement flat with care. Vanessa did a lot of living on the floor. They climbed the narrow staircase. In the hallway Hinkley saw that the hall door now had a mortise-lock fitted. There was no London Bar. It was probable that there were no hinge-bolts fitted. It was no more secure than it had been before the lock had been changed.

'Mother says you'll be in the spare room.'

This was a question of sorts.

'Yes.'

'She has it prepared for you.'

'Right.'

'We're both so glad you're here, Daddy. Now, I must fly.'

It was her turn to kiss him on both cheeks.

'Still seeing . . . er . . . .' Hinkley couldn't remember his daughter's boyfriend's name.

'Oh yes,' she replied. 'Now, I really must go.'

When she had left, Hinkley went upstairs with his suitcase. He stood in the master bedroom for some time. It was as he remembered it. He could find no trace of another man. It was entirely Mary's room. In the spare room he found a present from Mary parcelled up for him on the bed. He weighed it in his hands, squeezed it. Material folded. Clothes. Something with large buttons. He took it downstairs to the living room and opened it. Mary had bought him a coat in Cording's, the waterproofers of Piccadilly. She had correctly assumed that he would come to London unprepared for the miserable weather. Hinkley was prepared for most discomforts that befell him, but not the weather.

The coat was a wise choice on Mary's part. He had only brought a light mackintosh, and even now, in the house, he was feeling cold. He touched one of the radiators. It was warming up. He leant against it and held out the coat for inspection. It was a fine garment. He regretted not having brought his wife and daughter presents. True, he had left for London at short notice, but there had been time to get something at the airport. He had failed to be considerate.

He went to the drinks cabinet to pour himself a whiskey. There was a quarter-full bottle of Galliano on the middle shelf, just where a right-handed person would place a frequently used bottle. Mary didn't drink Galliano. Vanessa didn't like liqueurs. Who was the regular guest? Perhaps there was more than one who came to his freshly painted house to drink it. Perhaps Mary had developed a taste for liqueurs? He had noticed that there were no ashtrays. Had she given up smoking? Everything Mary and Jack did together seemed to end with them both smoking. Would their estrangement be complete when there was no longer a shared vice?

This room he was in had been his room without images, the room he had carefully hung with old maps and old or ancient text. Mary had altered it to include a pair of rococo oil paintings of powdered nymphs, a series of equestrian prints and a portraits of a nineteenth-century country gentleman.

The nominal husband, father, householder, switched off the lights, sat down with his whiskey and put his new coat across his lap. The curtains were parted. In the light from the street, his face shone like that of a policeman.

In this richly furnished room, the air seemed not to change but to remain a constant medium for scented dust and the voices of polite strangers. Somehow, the dust would appear thick in the mirror while the strangers, like vampires, would be invisible. Their voices lingered, as did Mary's perfume.

Hinkley sat still, breathed evenly and once again summoned for scrutiny the half a dozen decisions that had brought him to this impasse, half a dozen seminal decisions profoundly different to those that had steered Mary's life to the same point.

Hinkley waited patiently for Mary. Patience was one of his strengths. It would be a mistake, he thought, to brood over the distance between himself and the two people he loved, without first accounting for his selfishness. He needed to fix in his mind the moment he realised that he had been compromised. He needed to recall with absolute clarity the incident that marked the onset of his personal decline. It had started eighteen months earlier . . . or so it seemed.

It was a similar set of circumstances: he had been summoned to London at short notice. After his briefing, he was immediately returned to West Berlin, where he was stationed. The authorities had been making a series of arrests in West Berlin on the strength of information from an East German named Steibelt. The East Germans employed Steibelt in their documentation department, which, in addition to furnishing false documents, concerned itself with the larger task of creating legends for agents operating in the West. Steibelt was a nervous little man, but he was clever. Like Hinkley, he was good with files. His initial approach to the Americans, however, was clumsy. He had got tired of sitting alone in cafés waiting for someone to make contact. The CIA decided they didn't want anything to do with him. What he offered seemed too good for one so clumsy. He was a Quiet One. Moscow Centre liked to use homosexuals for the purpose of blackmail. They would have a thick file on Steibelt. Snitkina's lot would be paying him a little extra attention in case they might benefit from a personal relationship. The CIA suspected it was an attempt to plant a misinformer. They had had their share of them. They were playing safe.

MI6 saw it differently. They had been watching Steibelt too. They had him marked as a possible defector. They didn't mind him being nervous. He had always been nervous. His colleagues were used to his fidgety habits.

London proceeded with care. They gave him a modest shopping list: photographs of some low-grade documents.

Steibelt delivered.

They gave him another list. This time they said they wanted to borrow the documents.

Steibelt delivered.

Finally, an offer of money and, if necessary, asylum, was made and accepted.

Hinkley was appointed Steibelt's case officer. Steibelt was based in Leipzig. In order to reduce the risk of him being caught, Hinkley was directed to run him from West Berlin. There was to be no radio contact, no personal contact. Communication was to be maintained through a series of dead-drops. It was Hinkley's first big case. For a long time it worked without hindrance. It proved to be an excellent pairing of editors.

The information got better. It got so good, in fact, that the doubters – and there was a body of them at Century House – again called into question the authenticity of the material. They had not been able to discredit him, but they maintained that Steibelt's motives had not been adequately established, nor had his methods been properly vetted.

However, C remained confident of Steibelt's bona fides.

With the arrests in Berlin, the East Germans were looking for a traitor. Steibelt was under suspicion. He was called to Moscow for interrogation.

Hinkley returned immediately to Berlin, where, under instructions from London, he selected a senior East German officer to be gulled. Zeisler was the name of the man he chose. He was to be abducted and brought to the West in order that it might appear that he had, on hearing of the search for the traitor, fled, lest he be exposed. Zeizler was, in fact, a loyal and committed party member. Hinkley had chosen him for several reasons. Zeisler had served in the East German trade mission in Bonn. His weakness lay in his liking for low life. He liked to take trips to Hamburg and West Berlin to gather scraps of information, the value of which he liked to exaggerate to cover for his time fornicating. Zeisler had been marked as a potential target for blackmail. MI6 had photographs of him in a Hamburg club cavorting with a woman and an American named Baxter. Baxter worked for the CIA out of their technical warehouse in Washington. It was a common ploy to use Soviet and Eastern Bloc weapons and ammunition in assassination bids and CIA-backed coups. The stock had to be periodically replenished and updated. Baxter was on a buying mission. He had done his business. He was having some fun. He didn't realise it was a contrivance. He didn't know that this little flesh party included a senior officer in East Germany's Haupt-Verwaltung Aufklärung, operating in Bonn. He wouldn't have been expected to know. He was an assistant warehouse man in the armaments section. He didn't even know what the guys who made the lethal bacillus in another part of the warehouse looked like. It was extremely unlikely that Zeisler would have seen a photograph of the assistant warehouse man in Washington.

MI6 got a lot of lewd, sharp-focus photographs.

It was sound blackmail material. It was enough, perhaps, to turn Ziesler around. Hinkley now had good reason to thank the gods that the material had been filed pending the imminent retirement of the director of the HVA. With the arrival of his successor, Zeisler would be out of favour. The new man disapproved of Zeisler's lechery. It was believed that in the new regime Zeisler's loyalty would no longer go unquestioned. It was intended that the photographs be used to discredit Zeisler when the new appointment was made – an appointment which turned out to be less imminent than expected.

One of Hinkley's tasks was to ensure that the name of a bogus bank account in Zurich could be credited to Zeisler. This was done by the by planting incriminating evidence at the time of his abduction.

★

Zeisler was to be abducted from his summer-house in the woods near Possneck, 125 kilometres south of Leipzig. From Possneck it was only 25 kilometres to the frontier, but it was all uphill, and that stretch of the border was particularly well monitored. It was feasible to snatch Zeisler, but could they be sure of getting him out immediately? The coordinator of the clandestine operation – in this case, head of Berlin Station – was satisfied that they could, but insisted that they cross the frontier via an underground route which would take them through Czechoslovakia. It was about 80 kilometres from the summer-house to their point of crossing on the Czech border, then a further 130 kilometres to the West German frontier. In all, a journey of some 210 kilometres, part of which had to be done on foot.

It was a Saturday. Zeisler had left his wife and children behind in Leipzig for their summer house, where he was to meet his favourite prostitute. The sun was low in the sky, shining through the trees, by the time he got there. The woodland noises were sharp on the cold air. There was no prostitute to meet him, however. In her stead were two female agents, one with a pistol, the other with a syringe. They injected him and took him away, leaving behind a plain plastic ballpoint taken from a teller's desk in the bank in Zurich. His new friends had earlier marked the copy of the Leipzig telephone directory Zeisler kept in the summer house – on the first page of listings they had marked with a pinprick digits and letters that together constituted the bank code for the bogus Zurich account.

The two agents and their groggy prisoner rendezvoused with the man who was to take them across the Czech border. They crossed into Czechoslovakia on foot, as they were to do at the frontier with West Germany. Another man led them across the second frontier. It had cost a lot of money, and exposed friends to enormous risk, to have that tiny chink in the Iron Curtain open for just sixty seconds.

Hinkley was at the German frontier to meet them. He watched for them through binoculars from a hide half a mile from the fence. They were late. It was several minutes after the crossing before Hinkley could speak; before he could unlock his jaw.

Zeisler was taken to Munich. Unusually, C had sent his own man. It was he who conducted the Zeisler interrogation, most of it with just the two men in the room. After the interrogation, they dressed him in an expensive suit, silk shirt and tie, crocodile shoes, and gave him money to buy his minders drinks. They took him for walks, took him to clubs, generally showed him off to the HVA.

The risks taken were all for nothing. Neither the HVA nor Moscow Centre were convinced that Zeisler was their traitor. They believed he had been kidnapped. They had drawn up a short list of suspects, Steibelt among them, and called them to Moscow for interrogation. Moscow Centre taking charge in this German domestic affair pointed to the magnitude of the treachery.

Steibelt and the others were not under arrest. As far as they were aware, they had been called to assist in an enquiry. The brighter ones thought it was to submit a verbal report on their fellow officers in the light of the Berlin arrests. The brightest one, Steibelt, knew just how little time he had. Each of them was being watched closely. The Volga with the Chaika engine and concrete ballast in the boot was a constant companion. Nothing moved faster on the streets of Moscow.

Steibelt went for a steam bath and disappeared. Nothing was heard of him for more than a week. Berlin Station believed him dead, and assumed he had divulged all he knew. Everything had gone sour for Hinkley. Then, a man got on the U-bahn train on which he was travelling and sat down beside him.

'Mr Hinkley, I'm a friend of Dieter Steibelt,' he said. 'He wants you to know that he is in East Berlin. You must help him. There isn't much time.'

He spoke quietly and with clear diction. It was difficult to place his accent. *Czech, perhaps,* thought Hinkley. He had learnt his English from an Englishman, not an American. Hinkley had a dim recollection of having seen his face, but the candid approach had thrown him.

'*Mir lied, ich verstehen nicht,*' replied Hinkley with a bemused grimace.

'Please, Mr Hinkley,' said the man, continuing in the same low, earnest voice, 'no one there can help him. There isn't much time.'

Christ, thought Hinkley, looking at the man's reflection in the glass. *Klinovec. Major Klinovec.* He had seen a photograph of him on file. Deputy Head, Directorate S. On this U-bahn train addressing him by name. It was ludicrous. It couldn't be.

'It *must* happen today. It's in your hands.'

He waited for a response.

Hinkley said nothing.

The man got off at the next station.

Hinkley tried to follow him, but lost him soon after coming up onto the street.

Hinkley checked the files. The photograph wasn't as sharp as he remembered it. There was room for doubt. He reported the incident to Head of Station. He got a cool reception. It was put to Hinkley that the only possible explanation for such an approach was that Steibelt was still alive, that the HVA believed him to be hiding in East Berlin, waiting for his chance to cross, and that they wanted his case officer to draw him from cover.

'Well yes,' said Hinkley hesitantly, 'something like that.'

'You are now suggesting that the Deputy Head of Directorate S took it upon himself to arrange this personally.'

'Yes,' said Hinkley, even more doubtfully.

'Any one of a dozen of this bureaucrat's loafers could have made such an approaxch on his lunch-break.'

'It was Klinovec,' said Hinkley adamantly. 'I don't know why, but it *was* Klinovec.'

'How does he know you're Steibelt's case officer? Did you tell him?' The note of ridicule in his voice was clear.

Hinkley sent a message to East Berlin via the established dead-drop. The signal to collect was broadcast on American Forces Network radio as arranged. The drop was near the hundred-yard fence on the eastern side of the wall. It could be seen clearly with binoculars from the top of a newspaper office building in West Berlin. Hinkley kept watch. It was more than forty-eight hours before Steibelt came out of hiding to collect. They were waiting for him. They shot him dead in the street. Hinkley saw it from the office building through his binoculars. He saw Steibelt's body crumple on the ground. The crack of automatic fire was a little delayed, owing to the distance from his vantage-point. Hinkley was on his own when he witnessed it. It made him sick to his stomach. He had unwittingly betrayed the little fellow.

Now, sitting in his darkened room in Chelsea waiting for another telephone call, he found the whole package of revelations choking him. It *was* Klinovec who had approached him on the U-bahn train. In the light of events in Barcelona, it was clear that he *was* a double-agent run outside the network, perhaps answering to C alone. Steibelt had been his cut-out. Klinovec was the major source of intelligence, not Steibelt. In Moscow, Steibelt had gone to him for help. Klinovec had done as much as he could without incriminating himself. He had got him to East Berlin. He had risked a meeting in the West, but did not dare to use channels reserved for infiltrating agents into the West to get Steibelt out. Ultimately, Klinovec had ensured that Steibelt was shot rather than taken alive to save himself.

It was part of Hinkley's job to be passionless. The veins were never to stand out on his neck and wrists for any belief. That way, more business could be done. The awkward truth could be skilfully diluted. The unfathomable nature of desire was matched – whatever its depth – by the bottomless well of deception.

4

When Hinkley heard the key turn in the lock on the hall door he lowered his glass to the floor and got out of the chair. It didn't seem right to be sitting when Mary entered the room; not after so long an absence.

'Jack!' she called from the hall. 'Are you here, Jack?'

'I am.'

'What's happened to the lights?'

It hadn't occurred to him to switch on the lights in the living room.

Mary threw the switch.

'That's better. I thought for a moment the bally lights had gone too. You heard about the heating?'

'Yes. Vanessa told me. How are you, Mary?'

'I think I'm catching a cold.' She made a job of removing her coat. 'Imagine, we still have to have the heating on in the evenings. What's the matter?' she asked in response to Jack's formal, inspectorial look. 'Don't you like my hair? Better than it was, don't you think, darling?'

Hinkley felt the heat rise in his face. How the hell was he to know whether or not it was better than it had been? What game was she playing, pretending that they weren't separated?

'It suits you.'

'Well I know that, for goodness' sake,' she replied with practised kindness. 'Sorry I wasn't here for you. Did Vanessa meet you?'

Hinkley noted how well she dressed, how gracefully she moved. Her perfume was strong. When he first met her at Oxford, Mary, in spite of her anorexia, moved eloquently. She wore nice clothes and the same strong scent. His attentions had confused the melancholy undergraduate. She began to eat even less than she had been eating before they met. He repeatedly took her to dinner, even though she wouldn't eat. She couldn't refuse the invitations. He didn't know what else to do. Hinkley still saw the anorexia in her. She had never lost the melancholy air. Anorexia had kept her brightness in check.

'Yes. She's gone to meet what's-his-name.'

'You know his name, darling. It upsets Vanessa when you do that. It doesn't upset me.'

Hinkley made no reply.

Mary crossed the floor, linked arms with him, kissed him lightly on the cheek.

'To be honest,' she continued, 'I'm not mad about Roger either, but our daughter is, so we really ought to make the effort.'

'Must we?' he asked dryly.

He returned her kiss.

'He has brains. That should please you. Not like the last one. He had a flat head, remember? Like somebody had hit him with a spade.' Mary laughed. It was an attempt to dispel the tension.

Hinkley had had a colleague in Special Branch run a check on Roger. It didn't make much of a report – a public school twit bursting with confidence – two convictions for speeding in Daddy's car – family house in Kent – family had money – in spite of the speeding offences, Roger had been given his own sports car – he didn't pay parking fines, of which he had incurred many – no drugs charges.

'I've said I'd put them up in Barcelona if they want to visit. She's never been to Barcelona.'

There was the faint suggestion in his tone that his daughter had been discouraged from visiting, but Mary chose to ignore it.

'Sweet Jack,' she said sweetly, and planted another light kiss on his cheek, 'welcome back.'

Hinkley winced.

'Have you eaten?' she asked, walking to the kitchen.

'Yes, I have.'

'How *are* you?'

'Well. Yes, very well.'

She had had the kitchen redecorated. In her redecorated kitchen she looked enquiringly as he sat with one elbow resting on the table, scratching the day's growth on his face. He was older.

'You look well,' she said.

'It's bloody cold in England.' It was all he could think to reply. Then it occurred to him to thank her for her present, but she spoke again before he found the words.

'So they summoned you at short notice?'

The courtly disdain for the unpleasant affairs of state was familiar to Hinkley. Mary had from the outset indulged in that luxury conceit – the firm as mistress.

'Yes, they did. It'll be a short visit.'

Mary hummed while she made tea.

She had brought a newspaper home. It was on the table in front of Jack. The hijacking was front-page news.

'What an ordeal,' said Mary, seeing that he had begun to read the report. 'None of us is safe any more.'

Was it his imagination, or did Hinkley really detect an inference that he and his associates had again failed to protect the innocent?

Mary could hear her husband thinking. It was the sound of glass being ground on stone.

'Is that why you're in London?' she continued, indicating the newspaper report.

'Yes,' replied Hinkley distractedly. Only now had the full horror of the hijacking sunk in. There was a photograph of a plastic mortuary bag containing shoes and a box of spectacles waiting to be claimed. 'It can only be a short visit. I have to get back.'

Hinkley was trying to make it easy for both of them, and she was pretending that everything was normal between them: normal, that is, to the point of his occupying one of the spare bedrooms.

Wasn't she going to tell him she had had the locks changed? Was he to press the bell when he wanted to come in?

'Vanessa tells me there have been burglaries.'

'We were in a state of siege. We daren't have left the house unoccupied, but now, with the new locks . . . .'

'You should have let me do it. The house is no more secure than it was.'

Mary had not been expecting this reproach. Now it was Jack who continued without waiting for a response.

'You've had the decorators in,' he said accusingly.

'Yes,' said Mary guardedly. She was determined to meet one criticism at a time. 'What's wrong with the new locks?'

'It's not the locks,' said Hinkley shortly, 'it's the wood that gives around the lock. It must be reinforced. I'll see to it.'

'I've a set of spare keys for you.'

Spare keys . . . thought Hinkley.

Mary poured tea for one, for Jack.

He had been received as well as might be expected, given his own state of mind. He returned to the newspaper, to the photograph. It was another image, to add to the gallery of atrocities housed beneath some trap-door in his brain, a small, but increasing collection of images to which he was somehow party, they being either a starting point for an investigation, or the grisly conclusion to an operation.

Hinkley rose early the following morning, his body still on Spanish time. He hadn't slept well. Another plastic bag had been disgorged through the trap-door and lay on the floor of his brain. This one, a black refuse-sack, had Larch moving inside it as though he was a foetus.

Hinkley's thwarted operation had been at the expense of immediate intelligence-gathering on the tarmac at Barcelona Airport. Direct contact with Barcelona Station had been temporarily suspended as a result of his alarm call. With the investigation into Larch's murder, and the complication of a comprehensive report on the hijacking, which included liaison with other services, there was too much for Davis and Higgins to do. Officers from other stations would be sent. Hinkley realised that for a second time in his career he had lost control, not through incompetence, but rather as a result of extraordinary circumstances.

There was nothing he could do. He would have to wait until he could make his report to C. He would take advantage of the early-morning peace to clarify in his mind the sequence of events in the Barcelona of the previous forty-eight hours.

He made Earl Grey tea and, from the upstairs sitting room window, stepped out onto the narrow balcony – a catwalk with wrought-iron railings that ran the length of the terrace. It was an cold as the previous day had been. He noticed, however, that the pitch underfoot bore the imprint of plant buckets that attested to previous hot days. Mary had replaced the shrub-buckets with seasonal flowers in window-boxes. He could tell she had done it recently because the shallow circular grooves in the pitch had not yet weathered. Doubtless, she had asked the house-painters to be darlings and remove the buckets.

In the past year Hinkley had returned to London several times for meetings at Century House. On most of those brief visits he had chosen not to contact his family, partly because the visits were so brief; chiefly because it was the easier of two complex options. The measured telephone calls from Barcelona were a difficult enough performance. He had no desire to confront Mary's indifference at source without there being time enough for other more reasonable thoughts to assert themselves.

The order to wait for a call at his London home now had him longing to nurture whatever goodwill, not to say, love, that could be mustered between him and Mary.

★

'You look sick.' They were C's opening words.

'Just a little tired, sir,' Hinkley replied.

'Your operator, Larch. Knew him well, did you?'

'Yes, sir.'

'Is that why you're sick?'

'Not sick, sir. Just tired.'

'I expect Larch was tired when they caught him out.'

'Klinovec is one of ours, isn't he?'

They was no reply. He shouldn't have asked.

'You're blaming me for Larch's death? You're saying I shouldn't have sent him?' A mixture of guilt and anger had made Hinkley drop the "sir".'

'You should have waited for instructions.'

'There wasn't time. I had the bastard. He sold us down the river in Berlin. I wasn't told he was ours.'

Now Hinkley sounded bitter.

Another silence, then: 'Your actions have put me in an awkward position. Larch's death makes it worse. The Foreign Office has caught wind of your operation. They want to know what Larch was up to, and what games you and Higgins were playing at the airport. Lord Peacher's son was among those wounded. He died this morning. I've had the Foreign Secretary on to me personally. Am I to tell him and the Defence Intelligence Committee that while these fanatics were holding us to ransom, my men were out kidnapping one of our *own* agents?'

49

Hinkley made no reply. He could hear the old man breathe unevenly. He had stirred the anger in him with his impertinence.

It was now clear to Hinkley why C could afford to have been so generous in the allowances he had made for Hinkley's inexperience in Berlin. 'Is there to be an enquiry? Am I suspended?'

'Lockwood will call you. Until such time, I want you to rest.'

Suspended, thought Hinkley. Investigation already in progress. With Klinovec being run outside the network it would take time to make discreet enquiries and assess the damage.

'No one else must know about Klinovec,' C said solemnly, after an appropriate pause.

'Yes, sir.'

'You, of course, know nothing of the circumstances of Larch's death.'

'Yes, sir.'

'And Hinkley . . . .'

'Yes, sir?'

'If you want to seek out the wicked and see justice is done, you don't belong with us.'

The Barcelona office was yet to be cleaned, C told Hinkley. There was to be no communication with Davis and Higgins. C instructed Hinkley to stay in London until he was issued with orders from the Iberian Desk at Century House.

Hinkley left the car park on foot via the emergency staircase, which brought him up into Hyde Park. The sun was shining, but it was still cold.

★

Mary wasn't in the Chelsea house when Hinkley returned. She had told him the previous night that she was teaching English to Japanese businessmen. The money was good, although she didn't need to work. Family investments provided her with an adequate private income. She claimed she enjoyed the work. Her Japanese students insisted on being taught apart from other nationalities. She said they were formal, demanding, polite. Hinkley was glad she had a job. It was something they could talk about, although she wasn't forthcoming on the subject: she hadn't said where the classes were held; she had left no telephone number, no schedule.

Vanessa was also at work, or at lunch. Roger probably took her to lunch regularly.

Hinkley wanted something hot to eat. He thought of a fry-up. He hadn't had a fry-up since he had left for Barcelona. He decided on a take-away: chicken korma from the local Indian restaurant. The chicken korma had always been good.

On his way back from the restaurant, when he had turned the corner into what he called his lucky street, he saw a man waiting on his doorstep. From that distance he was a stranger. He had a suitcase. The suitcase was on the ground. His body-weight rested on one leg. He had been waiting a while. Hinkley needed to get closer. He kept his pace. The figure, although relaxed, was watchful. Hinkley couldn't avoid drawing his attention: he was the only pedestrian in the street. Hinkley was jumpy. He transferred the carrier bag containing the food to his left hand, and put his right hand in the pocket of his new coat. At twenty yards, he could identify him. He took his hand out of his pocket. The man had a sunny grin on his ruddy face that said: I've just played one of those silly familiar tunes on your doorbell.

'Jack! How are you, Jack?'

It was Mary's older brother. He could get two weeks out of that suitcase, thought Hinkley.

'Geoffrey!' Hinkley shook the outstretched hand. He didn't want to share Mary for the few days he would be in London, but a man with a suitcase was not easily discouraged.

'Didn't she tell you I was coming, Jack?'

'Yes, yes. Put your bag down. Come into the living room.' Hinkley was distracted. 'Have you eaten?' Suddenly, he didn't want anything himself. Adrenalin had soured his stomach.

Hinkley's jolly brother-in-law refused the chicken korma. He had more serious problems with his stomach. He was in London for tests, he explained. The Royal Marsden. Cancer.

'If it's bad news, they'll keep me in, operate as soon as they can. Whatever the results, I shan't be stopping long. I don't want to be in anybody's way.' He was smiling now. 'Besides, I've too much to do on the farm to worry about being sick.'

Hinkley turned the food onto a plate and forced himself to eat. Geoffrey's smile sickened him. He'd had enough of making a joke of misery growing up in Liverpool.

'Geoffrey. I *am* sorry,' Mary said when she came in. 'I should have been here but I got held up.' She kissed both men. There was something religious in her kissing, Hinkley thought.

'Not to worry, Mary. Jack's been entertaining me,' said Geoffrey.

'He's a darling,' Mary said, as though her husband was absent. 'You don't have to go to the hospital until tomorrow morning?'

'That's right.'

'Oh it *is* good to see you, Geoffrey!'

They embraced.

'I brought you eggs,' said Geoffrey. 'They're in the case.'

After she removed the eggs, Mary asked Jack to put her brother's suitcase in the guest room. There was only one serviceable guest room: the room Hinkley had slept in the previous night. The other spare bedroom was full of junk and had a broken window-pane. Hinkley was moved into his wife's bed by default.

Vanessa came home late. She brought her boyfriend.

'Roger and I have an announcement to make . . . .'

Fuck me, thought Hinkley.

'We're going to get married.'

'Wonderful!' exclaimed her mother.

'There's going to be no engagement. We'll get married from Roger's parents' house. We'll have the reception there, too.'

'That was quick!' said her mother.

'We've decided. That's how we want it.'

'This is simply wonderful news!' exclaimed her mother, looking to Jack. She was more excited than Vanessa.

'I very much want you to be there, Dad,' said Vanessa. 'That's one of the reasons we're doing it at short notice . . . .'

'Oh?' said her mother. 'What are the other reasons?'

'Don't be silly, Mother.'

'Next Saturday, at 3 PM, to be precise,' interjected Roger nervously.

'You *can* stay, can't you?' Vanessa asked her father.

'Some of the arrangements have already been made,' said Roger.

Fuck off, Roger. This is between my daughter and myself.

'Of course he can, can't you, dear?' said Mary.

Je-sus!

'I can try,' he replied weakly. 'I can't promise.'

Why does this come as a surprise to me, Hinkley wondered.

'Jack, don't be silly,' said Mary. 'You've *got* to be there.'

'*I'll* give her away!' interjected Geoffrey good-humouredly.

'I want you to be there, *too*, Uncle Geoffrey.'

'Wouldn't miss it for the world, pet.'

'And Uncle Paul,' added Vanessa. 'He must come too.'

Mary insisted upon an immediate domestic celebration. She regaled the company with the story of her marriage to Jack Hinkley. It was strange for Jack to hear her tell it. He caught himself nodding and smiling. He wanted to remember the wedding as she was now recounting it. Though not without affection, what he recalled was a nervous, snobbish affair. They had married for the sake of the child. He hadn't failed as a husband and father. He had fallen short. So far as he could tell, that was as bad, but there was no denying theirs had been a civilised union, albeit without an abundance of passion.

There were no crippling questions left unanswered. Mary and Vanessa were thriving in their own way without him, and he could cover for his weakness, the spinelessness in personal matters that he had inherited from his father.

That night he shared Mary's bed. It was less awkward than either had imagined it would be. Neither slept well. Both knew they would have slept less had they been apart.

Mary dreamed fitfully while Hinkley's mind spun. His world had been suspended. It was now confusing rather than complex. He should have been in Barcelona instead of here, holding Mary's fretful hand.

Why wouldn't C let him go back? He had got the message about Klinovec. He'd keep his mouth shut. What were they concealing from him?

5

'No, Higgins!'

Hinkley sprang out of bed convinced that Higgns had thrown up on Mary, on him, all over the bed. Hinkley couldn't stand it. It brought him back to the newspaper office building in Berlin, to his long vigil, the soldiers dropping down from the tail-boards of lorries, the shooting of Steibelt, his own retching.

He woke Mary. He told her he had had a nightmare. Told her to go back to sleep.

He went out for fresh air. His muscles tightened. The cold air scrubbed the inside of his lungs as if with a ship's brush. Soon, he was feeling better.

He walked by the river until his corner newsagents was open. He bought the the morning papers and went back to the house.

Although it was still pretty early, Geoffrey was wandering around the house, whistling breathily.

'Morning, Jack,' he said brightly. 'Been out for the papers, I see.'

'Yes.'

'I like a good read in the morning. After you, if I may?'

56

Geoffrey sounded as though he was on holiday.

'Yes, of course.'

Hinkley made tea for both of them. Geoffrey took his to his room when he saw that his brother-in-law was intent on reading his newspapers.

Hinkley withdrew to the living room. He read the papers by the yellow light coming through the closed curtains.

Following the previous day's reports of the Barcelona hijacking, the press led with the death of Lord Peacher's son. One newspaper went on to quote a 'reliable source' in the Foreign Office as having said that a hitherto unmentioned fourth member of the terrorist group had left the aircraft with the survivors and had escaped due to the incompetence of our own intelligence services.

Had some smart fucker in the Foreign Office pieced together inaccurate scraps of information fed to him from the consulate in Barcelona or through Madrid? Hinkley regretted having snubbed the consulate officials in the car park of the airport hotel. It had made them suspicious. There were those in the Foreign Office who wanted MI6 brought firmly under the control of the Foreign Office. They didn't want a strongman at its head. They wouldn't shrink from exploiting any opportunity to suggest that there was incompetence at every level in Century House. The incumbent C would be a hard one to topple. He had a better relationship with many politicians than he had with Foreign Office officials. His support was spread. He had as many friends in White's as he had in the Athenaeum Club.

It was possible that C had arranged for this story to be leaked. It would draw attention away from the facts. C would dismiss the story as a fabrication to the Defence Intelligence Committee. He would then have a separate story to cover Larch's death. Presumably, this version of events would corroborate the story Klinovec would tell his masters in Moscow. The inaccuracy of the British newspaper reports would lend credence to his story. It would be seen as another attempt by someone in the Foreign Office to discredit MI6. Moscow's ears in Whitehall would confirm this.

According to the newspaper, a crisis meeting of EEC Interior Ministers had been called at the request of Britain. The Home Secretary would chair a meeting of the European Counter Terrorist Organisation (TREVI) in London, scheduled for the end of the month, but now brought forward to the end of the current week. The article concluded by stating that there were moves to carry out preemptive raids involving the SAS and the German G9 force against terrorist cells in Europe. A decision as to whether or not these raids could be sanctioned would be taken by committee at the TREVI meeting.

Hinkley knew that preemptive raids such as those suggested had already taken place. A few had been successful. More had failed. Not that it needed to be made public. Politicians needed to be seen to be doing something to stop the terrorist. It was a dilemma for government and security services alike for, of necessity, many clandestine operations depended on secrecy for continued success.

Hinkley also knew that intelligence reports from the Middle East warned of two active terrorist groups at large in Europe, with a third preparing in Damascus, their targets to date, unknown. The fear in European capitals that there was about to be another spate of attacks was well founded. If there wasn't to be another hijacking, there would surely be shootings or bombings. There was talk of more bombs in Paris.

The weekend before the Barcelona hijacking, one of three sophisticated suitcase bombs had been stolen by an Israeli agent, and its carrier assassinated. The other two cases were still missing in Europe. An unprecedented hunt throughout the continent had yielded nothing. The suitcase bombs could be primed at any moment. It seemed utterly incongruous to Hinkley that his job for the day was to call on his brother, Paul, to invite him to his daughter's wedding.

Jack's younger brother, Paul, had always been popular with his contemporaries. He hadn't shone academically, but he was the best footballer in the school, and he could make his friends laugh. He rarely mitched classes. By and large, he stayed out of trouble. When he *was* in trouble, he most often talked his way out of it. From school, he had gone to art college to exercise and improve a mediocre talent. After foundation year, they put him in lettering. He was going to be a graphic artist. He left the art college without a diploma and went to London to become a photographer. He spent what little money he had saved on the cinema. He wore out his welcome with old school friends from Liverpool on whose couches he slept. They were only marginally better off than he was, having found a dry squat. He searched in vain for

a position as photographer's assistant. Optimism quickly
gave way to despondency. He stopped playing football. His
wit soured. Eventually, he got a job working with a por-
nographer. Paul was destined to be one of those never to
get past the first rung on the ladder. He stood somewhere
between the forty-year-old newspaper sellers and the age-
ing buskers.

There was an irony in Jack's relationship with his
brother, for of the two, Jack, the one who mitched so many
classes, had pursued academic background. He was the one
who avoided home life in so far as it was possible, but also
the one who knew about their parents' disaffection, about
their affairs. Jack had inherited their father's spinelessness
in personal matters; Paul had inherited the despondency
that went with it, that pervaded all he undertook. Paul had
remained ignorant of his parents' plight. He still wrote
regularly to their mother in Liverpool compounding the
lie that he was a successful fashion photographer. He sent
her expensive presents, which he could ill afford. He had
spent years in the company of small-time Soho villains yet
had essentially remained innocent, forever popular.

Jack had misgivings about visiting his brother. Why not
maintain the silence between them? They had never been
close. It had never been a close family. They had little to say
to each other. So far as he knew, Paul was still in a rut and
there was nothing he could reveal about his own work. If
anything, his visiting would be a source of embarrassment
to Paul.

Jack wanted to help his brother, but he couldn't help with
a job. Paul had gone too far along his chosen road for that kind
of help. Perhaps he could get him some freelance work. That

is, if he was still in the photographic business: Paul would lie to save face. Even if he was still in photography, Jack didn't know many photographers. Those he did know were the kind who took photographs of Paul and his villain associates.

Jack had been the star from the start. Their parents had thought if either boy were to go to art school it would be Jack. After all, Jack was adept at forging signatures.

Jack had offered his brother money many times. His offers had been purposefully flat, but still, they were all rejected. He decided he would take Paul to lunch and make another offer – as though it were the first.

Jack's brother lived in a damp basement in Nottinghill An overpriced bedsitter with basement-hall kitchen and coal-cellar bathroom. Much of the natural light was obscured by the landlord's car, which was parked most often in front of the basement window. The two hardy ivy plants Paul kept on the mantelpiece were more sick than the office plants in Barcelona. Everything in the flat was hopelessly damp.

It was a long time before Paul came to the door. Jack identified himself through the closed door. Eventually, Paul unlocked and opened it. He was in a terrible state. Jack groaned pitifully when he saw him. Paul's lip was cut and swollen. A front tooth was chipped. He had been mugged forty-eight hours prior to Jack's visit. He was on his own in that rotten basement. There was nobody to nurse him. Tears welled in his eyes when he saw Jack.

'Please, Jack, just go. I'm all right. Just go. Please go.'

Jack wouldn't go. He put his hand on his brother's shoulder, turned him and walked his back into the flat.

Paul told him about the mugging while he examined the wounds. It gave Jack the shivers. He had no stomach for wounds or deformities. The sight of blood made him squeamish, but he persevered with the examination.

'Paul, what have they done to you?'

Jack wasn't a fighter. He was concerned with information, footnotes, cross-references. Jack, like most of his fellow intelligence officers, was a reserved, watchful man; a man for whom the self-defence course at the nursery was an arduous and humiliating experience. In this instance, however, a professional coldness did not cool a desire for revenge. There was, of course, little chance of the muggers being caught.

'I've had it with this city, Jack. I'm getting out.'

Panic was gathering in Paul's throat.

Jack held his brother's hand across the table.

'Have you seen a doctor?'

'Yes. And the dentist. The dentist can fix this.' He pointed to his mouth with a stiff hand. 'They *can* fix it,' he said, as much to reassure himself as to reassure his brother.

'I know they can,' replied Jack. 'Did anybody help . . . at the station, I mean?'

'No.'

'It's all right. It's over. You did well.'

'I'm getting out, Jack.'

'I understand. You must get well first.'

'I'm getting well, Jack. The dentist can fix this. The swelling is almost gone.'

'To Liverpool?'

'No. Not there. Never back there.'

'You're right. You must get out of London. To the country. Somewhere quiet. Even for a short time.'

'Quiet. Yes. That's it.'

'Let me help.'

'Thanks for talking, Jack.'

'No. Let me do something. Stay in Chelsea tonight.'

'No. I've got someone calling.'

Jack knew that there was no one calling. Paul had been expecting no visitors when Jack identified himself through the door. There was no evidence of a partner. Paul was living on his own.

Paul changed the subject. 'What do you think of this dump, then? It took me a while to get this far.'

'How much does it cost?'

'Fifty quid a week.'

Jack scoffed.

'Not counting the bills,' Paul added. 'That's London for you.'

'Are you making out all right?' Jack asked solemnly. It was the nearest he would get to asking his brother if he was working.

'I always get by, Jack. You know that.'

Paul was afraid his brother might pry, so he forced the conversation further.

'My gas bill is low. I've found a way to fix it. It's an old meter. Come here. I'll show you.'

Jack followed his brother the few steps to the kitchen, Paul had to close the drop-down door of the dresser so that they could pass through to the pokey bathroom. Jack noted that his brother's diet – judging by what was on display – consisted mainly of porridge, bananas, fresh vegetables and liver. As cheap diets went, it was a nutritious one. It was some small indication that Paul had not given up on himself.

'See,' said Paul, standing awkwardly in front of the meter, 'I put a powerful magnet on the gauge. Stops it going round. He's on to me, though . . . the landlord. He knows I'm doing something, but he doesn't know what. He's had the gas man down to check the meter, but the meter is all right, isn't it. He's having a new meter put in. It'll be all plastic, won't it.'

'If you're still here when the plastic one is installed, I'll show you how to fix it with the vacuum cleaner,' said Jack, trying to sound practical. It was better than offering Paul money to pay his gas bill.

Paul smiled. It hurt him.

Jack saw one of those push carpet-sweepers in a corner of the bathroom. He realised that his brother probably didn't have a vacuum cleaner.

They went back into the bedsitting room. They were both stuck for somewhere to stay.

'How are Mary and Vanessa?' Paul asked. The second name caused him more pain from the lip-wound.

'They're both well,' replied Jack, as he moved to the window. 'Both asking for you. Vanessa is getting married. She wants you to come to the wedding.'

Paul was glad of some family news. 'When?'

'Next Saturday.'

Paul's surprise lost its warmth. 'I can't go, Jack. Not like this.' He smiled again, but this time with caution. It still hurt. 'Married, eh? I'll send her something nice.'

Jack swallowed hard.

'I know it's short notice but you'll be a lot better by Saturday. She really wants you to come.'

'All right,' Paul said. He had no intention of attending the wedding in anything like the state he was in. Jack knew it.

'You could say it was an accident if you don't want to . . . tell what happened.'

'What's her young man like?' Paul asked, in order to distract.

'Well, she likes him,' Jack replied evasively.

Paul nodded.

There was another pause. Jack looked out at the landlord's car. The registration plate was at forehead-height. The car had been washed recently. Jack's figure was hideously reflected in the underside of the fender.

Paul searched for something else to say.

'The landlord's wife – they lived upstairs, you see – she complained about my taking down the net curtains on that window. I had to take them down. There's no bloody light otherwise. I have to put them back up before I leave. They can't go back up crumpled, she says. She expects me to iron them.'

'Where are they?'

'The curtains?'

'Yes.'

'In the bottom of the wardrobe. Why?'

'How does she know they're crumpled?'

''Cause they're in the wardrobe, I suppose.'

'Did you tell her they were in the wardrobe?'

'No.'

'How does she know they're not folded neatly under the bed?'

'Fuck me. She's been in here snooping around.'

'You must get out of this place, Paul. Come and stay in Chelsea. Just for a few days. You must concentrate on getting well. You need a rest.'

'Jack, I'm all right. Just as soon as the dentist does this work, I'll get out of London.'

There was another pause. Then Paul asked: 'How long are you here for, then?'

'I'll stay for the wedding.'

'You don't look like you've come from Spain, but then you're probably not really working there at all, are you?'

'Vanessa says I look like I've always lived in Spain. I'm still in Barcelona.'

'That's nice,' Paul muttered.

There was yet another pause.

'Awful business, that hijacking. All those people killed,' said Paul abstractedly.

'Yes. Yes it was.'

Another pause.

'Will you be visiting Liverpool?' Paul asked. 'Visiting Liverpool' was his way of asking if he was visiting their mother.

'No.'

'She asked about you . . . . I ring sometimes.'

Jack wanted to take his brother out to lunch or, if his injuries forbade eating, for a drink. If not for a drink, for a walk. Anything to get him out of that horrible basement. Paul had committed himself to the lie about there being a visitor expected. He could not be persuaded to leave a note on his door for the phantom. Suddenly, it was time for Jack to leave.

'Forget everything else,' Jack advised. 'Just get well.'

'I will, I will,' replied his brother.

They embraced: something they had never done before. It was difficult for them both.

Jack printed his Barcelona address and telephone number on a scrap of paper and pressed it into his brother's hand.

'Call me. Come and visit me. It's a beautiful city. You should see the Catalan women.'

Jack gave an artificial sigh. He was over-anxious.

'Just telephone. I'll arrange for the ticket.'

'I'll get there. I'll get my teeth fixed, then I'll thumb a lift, if I have to.'

They parted.

Jack hurried away, knowing that his brother would not come to Barcelona.

He had been deeply disturbed at finding Paul battered and despairing. There was an irony in his protecting the nation from hostile regimes and his brother being brutally beaten in a London Tube station for a cigarette. He saw the random attack as a bad omen.

Jack Hinkley had strength of purpose. He believed in his work. It was his job to provide analysts with information from the field. Imbalance could be addressed with calibrated measures and seeds of doubt sown to make the opposition mistrust their own sources. Was it not surprising that a man with Hinkley's skills was, like his errant brother, forever caught between regret and desire. He was a man privy to more of reality than most. Being given to superstition was a new development.

★

The house in Chelsea was deserted. Mary was at her class, Vanessa at the opticians where she worked, and Geoffrey was being tested for cancer.

There was no message on the telephone answering machine.

Hinkley had a stiff drink. He decided to read. Reading a novel would calm him. He would then go for a long walk. The walk that morning had done him good. In Barcelona he walked whenever time permitted. He would mingle with tourists and traders in the Barrio Gotico. He would go from one bookshop to another, spending a considerable amount of time in each. Then, with whatever books he had bought, he would wander the dingy, overcrowded neighbourhood around San Pablo del Campo and the Paralelo district beyond. He liked the rhythm of those streets, the strong odours, the family scenes spilling out of doorways. It was in one of these streets that an angry young woman had insisted he take the cat she carried by the scruff of its neck. In each of the cities in which he had lived, Hinkley had done much the same. He had always been a reader and a walker. When he was a child, his father encouraged him to read. The encouragement did not come in a direct form, nor was it given by example. His father told him stories in which he passed himself off as a principal character. Stories he had adapted from his own indiscriminate reading. He told Jack he had met Hitler. Hitler, he said, had lived in Liverpool. Hitler, he said, had been a regular on his Green Goddess. He and Hitler had got talking. They discovered they shared an interest in maps and horses. They had gone to the races together, he said. Even though Jack knew that books and newspaper were his father's source, he could not but believe that at least part of each story was true. Not knowing which part was true brought Jack pleasure. It meant that any part might be true. It was this ability to exploit doubt in others that he wished to imitate.

As for walking, Jack had few friends. He and his classmates mitched school to go to the cinema. More often, he mitched by himself. He was content walking the streets alone. He would take care to avoid his father's bus route. Otherwise, he wandered the city incessantly. The streets and their doorways consumed him.

Hinkley couldn't concentrate on the novel. Geoffrey soon returned from the hospital. He had had his first batch of tests. He had stopped to buy groceries in Waitrose on his way back. He didn't want to have to eat more chicken korma. He whistled his way into the kitchen. He took items out of the bag one at a time, interrupting his whistling to read the labels out loud, searching for a place for each item in the fridge, in cupboards. Hinkley went for his walk sooner than he had planned.

Paul's disfigured face haunted him. Hinkley used to think that his brother would grow up like 'Uncle' Frank, the cinema-owner. Frank, he thought, couldn't be tricked, knew everything there was to know about street-life. He used to think he would be safe with Frank even down the worst piss-alley in Liverpool.

When attendance dropped at Frank's cinema he took to selling potatoes from a lorry to supplement his income. It started as a favour – filling in for a mate – but he saw how lucrative it could be. Potatoes sold wholesale door to door along the terraces and around the new housing estates. Frank blamed television for bad business at the cinema. His recognition of the new medium as the mass entertainment of the future, together with his entrepreneurial spirit, won Jack's mother's undying admiration. Her approval stretched to her insistence that Jack help him on the potato-round in the summer holidays. Paul was to help, too, but he just never showed up. In reality, Frank was a lazy bastard. He had never paid much attention to the programming for the cinema. He had let the building fall apart. As part-punishment for his infidelity, Frank's wife conspired in the cinema's neglect. Frank wasn't too proud to get his hands dirty. So Jack's mother said. Frank was full of good ideas. He had imagination – that was the conceit.

Keeping customers short-changed required a lot of paperwork and concentration. Frank confined himself to the lorry cabin. Jack did the donkey work. There was a few bob pocket-money and the cinema-pass that was eventually issued, and for which he was expected to be eternally grateful.

For a boy in his early teens, Jack had been unnaturally tolerant of unsatisfactory situations. That tolerance, which he had never lost, was now being stretched to its limit.

Part Two

1

In a cemetery in Leipzig, Steibelt's widow put flowers on her husband's grave. It was, so far as she knew, the anniversary of his death.

In Barcelona, the bodies of the three terrorists were released for burial.

In Moscow, Klinovec's thigh-wound had gone septic. He had removed the broken needle himself with an unsterilized tweezers.

In Whitehall, Lord Peacher was in private meeting with the Foreign Secretary. He claimed to have proof that the order to attack the hijacked British Airways jet in Barcelona had come from Century House. He demanded a full enquiry.

At Lord's cricket ground England was losing again. C, seated by the window, contemplated the Dresden and Leipzig arrests. The London-mole theory had gained credence, though as yet there was nothing concrete. He would have to be patient and guard against phantoms. It had become one of a number of nauseating worries. Again, he was called to the telephone. He was briefed in the car on his way to Century House. A bomb had exploded in a crowded restaurant in Paris, killing seven people and injuring many more. It was believed that the bomb was one of the two missing suitcase devices. There was reason to believe that the other missing case had passed into Britain through Heathrow.

In Damascus, MI6 Station Head was making his report to London. The third terrorist group had left the city: three on board an Air Maroc jet bound for Tangiers, the other two on a flight to Tripoli.

In Peter Jones's department store in Chelsea, Hinkley was looking for a wedding present, thinking about Klinovec, about Snitkina, about his cat.

Hinkley didn't find a wedding present. Now, walking back to the house he was thinking about Zeisler, too. It was now clear why C's man had been sent from London to Munich to interrogate Zeisler. It was clear why much of the interrogation took place with just the two men in the room. The interrogation was undertaken primarily to ascertain whether or not Klinovec was deceiving C. It was likely that not even Pickering, C's deputy, knew about Klinovec. There was no transcript, no computer record, no audio-tape of that interrogation to be found in Century House. Hinkley had looked for it when he returned to London shortly after the Zeisler operation had fallen apart. How blind he had been! How stupid not to have made the connection once Klinovec had approached him on the U-bahn in Berlin.

Geoffrey opened the hall door before Hinkley had his key in the lock. He said he had seen Jack coming down the street. Geoffrey had returned from his second batch of tests with another bag of groceries and his jolly, tuneless whistle. Now that the preliminary tests had been done, they wanted to cut out a piece of the growth to examine under a microscope. While Geoffrey made tea Hinkley rewound and played the telephone answering-machine. Only one message had been left. Peter for Mary. Please would she return the call.

Who was Peter?

★

In White's that evening, Lord Peacher stopped C on the staircase with a declamatory cry of 'You, sir!' He told C that he held him personally responsible for the service's part in the gross mis-handling of the hijacking in Barcelona. He warned that he had insisted upon an exhaustive enquiry into MI6's role in events.

C lit a cigar, formally offered his sympathy on the death of the peer's son, and continued up the stairs.

Early the following morning, C was summoned to the Foreign Office. An irate Foreign Secretary pointed out that he had been unable to brief the Home Secretary regarding the extent of MI6's involvement in the storming of the jet in Barcelona before he took the chair at the TREVI meeting because *he*, the Foreign Secretary, had not been briefed on the matter.

C replied that intelligence had been passed to the Spanish authorities and that Barcelona Station had been alerted.

What the hell was the fourth-man business, the Foreign Secretary asked.

There was no fourth man, C replied bluntly.

How was the death of this man, Larch, tied into the hijacking, asked the Foreign Secretary.

There was no connection, replied C.

That is not what I have been told, said the Foreign Secretary.

You must take *my* word for it, C insisted.

★

In Downing Street, Lord Peacher was having a private audience with the Prime Minister.

By midday, there was still no further clue as to where the third suitcase bomb may be in Britain. There were now doubts that it had passed through Heathrow.

In Tangiers, agents had lost track of the three suspected terrorists recently arrived from Damascus. Their associates in Tripoli, however, were still under surveillance. They had been given new clothes. They were now dressed like businessmen.

That afternoon, C attended a hastily arranged meeting called by the Prime Minister. The venue was Chequers. There was an afternoon tea spread.

'Malcolm.'

'Prime Minister.'

'Do sit down.'

'Thank you.'

'Our Doctor Edgeborne tells me you are unwell,' said the Prime Minister, pouring tea.

'Rheumatism, Prime Minister,' said C, pouring milk.

'You've been sitting in the grass at Kenwood, haven't you?' the Prime Minister said, putting the correct number of sugar-lumps in C's cup. 'What was the last programme you attended?'

'Tchaikovsky, Symphony Number 1 in G minor . . . and Marche Slav with fireworks.'

This seemed to come as a disappointment. A bubble had been burst. 'Mm.'

'I've had the Foreign Secretary in with me, Malcolm. I expect you know why.'

'Yes. Lord Peacher is claiming that I ordered the assault on the British Airways jet at Barcelona Airport.'

'Did you?' Sandwich offered.

'Yes, Prime Minister.' Sandwich refused.

'Why were there no negotiations?'

'The leader of this group was mentally unstable. He had killed before in similar circumstances in spite of his demands being met. He had already committed acts of violence on board the jet. Our surprise assault saved lives.'

'There was considerable confusion, was there not?'

'There was, Prime Minister.'

'Lives were lost as a result.'

'That was not our fault, Prime Minister. It was a British jet. The majority of passengers were British. That is why the Spanish consulted us. It was on the basis of our own intelligence that I ordered the attack. Any delay would have cost more lives. The confusion on the ground was their fault.'

'You refused to discuss the matter with the Foreign Secretary. You have not found a friend in him? I can't have this rift between the Foreign Office and Century House widening. There is no room for antipathy.'

'I am answerable to you, Prime Minister, not to the Foreign Secretary.'

'In the last resort, yes. You realise the position you have placed me in? If one says anything, one must say more.'

'Indeed.'

'There is to be an emergency debate on terrorism. The incident will be foremost on the agenda. The crusading press believes there is a political scandal to expose. You must give me information that will help me make the right decision, that will let me measure the consequences.'

'The facts are as written in the report, Prime Minister.'

'I have a delinquent Head of MI6, Lord Peacher says, and he is not alone in this view. There are claims of incompetence on the part of your team in Barcelona. It has been said you let one escape.'

'I'm not concerned with what Lord Peacher says, Prime Minister. It is regrettable that innocent people died. There was no fourth man, Prime Minister. I must tell you now, we anticipate further attacks in the near future.'

'More hijackings?'

'Perhaps that, too. Our current information suggests a bombing campaign.'

'To be carried out in Britain alone?'

'Possibly.'

'Possibly?'

'We now face obscure groups that have formed loose alliances. This is their strength.'

'Their paymasters remain the same, do they not?'

'Yes, Prime Minister, but they obey their bankers only if it suits them.'

'Are you telling me you haven't the resources to defeat this new ... super-breed? Do they not recruit from the same camps? If it is more money you need, say so. You know I am committed to a large increase in the Secret Vote.'

'Financial resources is *part* of it, Prime Minister . . . .'

The Prime Minister interrupted. 'Find a man's strength and you have found his weakness,' the Prime Minister said assertively. 'Strength is consistent. You can rely on it. You can manipulate it. Weakness is far less predictable. Come now, Malcolm, have you lost your taste for the task set you? *That* I find hard to believe.

C briefed the Prime Minister as to the new developments regarding the explosion in the Paris restaurant, the three terrorist cells at large in Europe, the third suitcase bomb. He outlined the measures that Century House was taking in conjunction with MI5, and C13, the anti-terrorist squad. The Prime Minister listened with a hard countenance.

C left Chequers, making a mental note to change his doctor.

2

'Jack, could you ring me at . . . .' The genial male voice, which did not identify himself, recited a number which was familiar to Hinkley. The voice, however, he did not recognise.

Hinkley switched off the answering-machine and left the house. He took an 11 bus to Victoria Station so that he could make his call from a public telephone outside his immediate neighbourhood.

It was about six o'clock in the evening. Geoffrey's tests had revealed cancer, but the cancer was benign. They would operate to rid him of it. Geoffrey, Mary and Vanessa were celebrating a benign cancer and an imminent wedding. Hinkley felt strangely disconnected. He thought the call he was about to make might be the one to get him out of a private hole. He thought it might put an end to his waiting.

'Jack Hinkley.'

'Smithers here. Despatch. Were you expecting a parcel care of Box 850?'

'No.'

'Thought not. No memo.'

'What have you got?'

'Brown paper parcel, posted Paris, Fifth Arrondisse-ment, Monday.'

'Come on, what's in it? I *know* you've had a look.'

'We *did* x-ray it. No memo, you see.'

'What's in it?'

'Pair of shoes, old boy.'

'Is there a note?'

'Couldn't see any.'

'Open it.'

'One moment.'

There was a short silence.

'Right. One pair of shoes, black, Crockett & Jones, size nine, worn but well kept, not more than three months old, I'd say, judging by the creases in the leather. The maker's stamp is still visible. Black fluff in the toe-caps, a bit smelly. No note. Nothing special about the brown paper. Want me to take them apart?'

'No.'

'Know what it's about?'

'Yes,' said Hinkley, drawing the corners of his mouth apart.

'Will you be collecting them?'

'Yes.'

'Oh good,' said Smithers dourly. He only used his genial voice when he thought someone outside the firm might hear. 'Bye-bye.'

When Hinkley put down the receiver he laughed out loud. Davis's shoes. Klinovec had had the gall to return Davis's shoes by post. In the middle of a crisis that seemed very amusing to Hinkley.

★

Klinovec wasn't easily unnerved. In Moscow, he was relaxing at the Turkish baths. He liked to walk as much as he liked to sit or lie flat within its confines. He liked to slap his feet on the marble. He bade good-day to familiar faces. Kremlin officials, a general, a military intelligence officer. He knew their laughter, their whisperings, their blemishes. Of most of them, he knew their drinking habits, their whoring. He drank and whored with them in safe-houses in Moscow and Gorky, even though he had an appetite for neither. In their company he felt safe from the current purge within the KGB. Such was the extent of the purge that LINE KR, normally responsible for the vetting and reassessment of staff abroad, had been engaged domestically as well. Indeed, there was cause for Klinovec congratulating himself on his using Snitkina, one of the chief investigators, to escape from Barcelona. Local KGB officers had killed to protect him. He was sure he had got away with the deception in Barcelona. If he hadn't – if he had been seen with the British agents, Hinkley and Davis – there was the contingency plan C had concocted.

After his rubdown Klinovec sat in an alcove. The stress of the previous week had exhausted him. However, it seemed to have no other effect. He was comfortable but for his thigh and his throat, both of which were bruised. A small area around the site where he had crudely parted the skin with tweezers had discoloured. The septic wound, though small, remained painful. It was still sore for him to swallow.

It wasn't easy to unnerve Klinovec, but the man who sat beside him was a most unexpected intruder.

Mikka was an old friend from Prague. As a young man, he had served without distinction in the Czech intelligence service, alongside Klinovec. Now he was a scavenger, a parasite wandering Europe, crossing from East to West unchallenged, travelling on tickets paid for by others. Klinovec knew him to be an indiscriminate peddlar of gossip and lies to agents and journalists. Neither side trusted him, or rather, both mistrusted him equally. He was a common pest out for as much as he could get for himself. That was why both sides used him as a go-between, a some-time agent-broker arranging swaps on the Glienicker Bridge in Berlin, or across some such divide. There were people like him travelling between east and west Beirut, between Baghdad and Tehran – wherever there was conflict. They were neither legitimate diplomats nor lawyers. They were clever, whining little shits performing a useful, if costly service.

'Josef!' he said warmly to Klinovec.

Klinovec, immediately suspicious, replied to the greeting with equal warmth.

'I was hoping you'd be here,' Mikka said. 'You are an extremely difficult person to find.' He chuckled.

Klinovec didn't like the chuckle.

'You never called me,' Mikka continued.

'I haven't been in Prague for a long time,' Klinovec said cordially.

'Oh?' said Mikka, pretending to know otherwise.

Klinovec called his bluff.

'When were you there last, Mikka?'

'You know I've moved?' he asked, pretending to be surprised.

'Mikka can always be found,' said Klinovec. 'Someone will have a number for you.'

'Come and have dinner with me.'

'I wish I could, but I can't. We must make a date.'

'It's good to see you, Josef.'

'Losing your hair, I see,' replied Klinovec.

'I must insist we have dinner.'

'And you're eating too much.'

'You're too hard on me, Josef.'

'Fat and balding.'

'You can choose the restaurant.'

'You want to speak to me?'

'Of course I do.'

'Who told you I was here?'

'I came here yesterday. And the day before. I heard you were in Moscow. I thought you might be here. You brought me here once, a long time ago. Don't you remember?'

'I remember.'

'It *is* good to see you, Josef. How are your father and mother? Do you see them often?'

'I haven't been to Prague for a long time. Remember?'

'Of course.'

'We can talk here,' said Klinovec.

'I want to celebrate!' exclaimed Mikka. 'Who knows when we might meet again? People who work in Dzerzinsky Square are, unlike myself, very difficult to see.'

Mikka's playful innocence was really annoying Klinovec now.

'Let me dress.'

He left Mikka in the alcove to pick at himself.

'Don't you have a driver?' Mikka asked brazenly in the street. 'Don't they give you a car?'

'I can get one if I need it.'

Mikka scoffed.

'We'll take mine.'

'Let's walk.'

'I don't usually walk,' Mikka warned.

'It shows.'

They gained several hundred yards on foot.

'What restaurant are you taking me to?' Mikka asked. Already he was struggling to keep up with his friend.

'I thought we'd wait a while.'

'Oh you did, did you?'

'I'm listening.'

'I'm hungry.'

Mikka bought a paper cone of fried sardines. Klinovec didn't buy any. Mikka didn't offer to share his. He ate greedily as they walked. Nothing was said. Mikka just made appreciative animal noises until the cone was empty.

He wiped his fish-soiled mouth and fingers with a silk handkerchief, which he drew from his sleeve. He had been watching two young women walking ahead of them, their little fingers linked. He had leered at them as they passed. They had not responded. They were both wearing their best stockings. They had dates with their boyfriends. They weren't interested in an avaricious little ferret like Mikka.

'These Moscow women, they are cold,' he proclaimed. He returned his handkerchief to his sleeve. 'I'm thirsty,' he complained. He was acting like a disgruntled pilgrim.

They stopped at a drink vending machine.

85

'Do you have any change?' he asked Klinovec.

Klinovec fed the machine a coin. Yellowish fluid squirted into a disposable cup. Mikka drank all of his state lemonade without pausing for breath.

'This stuff really is disgusting,' he said, looking painfully into the drained cup. 'Don't the tourists complain about it? I need a coffee.'

They went to the Ararat Café in nearby Neglinnaja Street. A small party of Americans huddled near the door. There were a few Germans. A few Finns. The rest were Muscovites.

'Bloody Western tourists,' complained Mikka in Czech, surveying the crowded interior in search of a free table. 'Look how the black-marketeers inspect their shoes to make sure they're from the West.'

There was no conviction in Mikka's voice.

'What favour do you want from me?' Klinovec asked bluntly – also speaking in Czech.

'Favour? Oh, not a favour, Josef. This is hopeless. We can't relax. Shall we go to your apartment?'

'We came here to drink coffee.'

'Yes, but look at the place: crammed with idlers.'

'We can go somewhere for a drink.'

As Klinovec turned to leave the café, a table became vacant.

'Ah!' said Mikka, pointing. 'Let us say a coffee, *then* a drink.'

They took their place at the table.

Mikka began to speak with nostalgia of their teenage years spent together in Prague. They had been friends because they were among a handful of youngsters in the same neighbourhood who were mad for jazz. Mikka had got the coveted job in the music shop. Klinovec had gone to university.

Klionvec didn't swallow this nostalgia crap. He didn't believe Mikka was sincere. They both knew that post-war Prague was an abysmal place. They were hard times.

Klinovec watched Mikka shape his spluttering lips about his cup. This was not a man whom anyone indulged with favours. What was his game? What would be the proposition? Was he selling scraps? Smuggling refugees? He was a fool if he thought Klinovec would get involved.

'Well?' said Klinovec, cutting short some drivel Mikka was delivering.

'Well what?'

Klinovec got up from the table and walked out of the café. Mikka followed clumsily. By the time he had got to the door, Klinovec was on the other side of the street.

'I want to talk to you about Herr Steibelt,' Mikka called after him.

He crossed the road carelessly. A militiaman's whistle blew in his wake. The militiaman caught up with Mikka and halted him. Klinovec had now disappeared. Mikka protested to the militiaman in Czech. He played the dazed tourist. He got off with a half-hearted caution.

Mikka hurried down the street. Klinovec was waiting for him around the corner.

'Who?'

Mikka was flustered. He was sweaty.

'Herr Steibelt. You know . . . the one from Leipzig. The one they caught in Berlin.'

'What are you talking about?'

'The traitor. The one they shot. Steibelt. You knew him.'

Klinovec resumed walking. Mikka kept pace, with difficulty.

'You *did* know him,' Mikka insisted. 'That's what I wanted to see you about.'

He had regained his composure in spite of the pace.

Klinovec went into a half-basement liquor store. He bought a bottle of vodka to drink on the premises. They stood at the ledge that ran along one wall.

'I know you spent time with him,' Mikka continued in Czech. 'He was a nice young man. Not particularly handsome, but well mannered.'

'What are you saying, Mikka?'

'I'm not suggesting there was anything more than sex between you. For all I know, you might have been feeding him lies. You see, he came to me in Berlin: as you said, I'm easy to find. He wanted me to get him out. He was panicking. I, of course, would have nothing to do with him. I don't deal in fugitives. I *did* follow him, however . . . all the way to Moscow . . . to the baths . . . to you. Then he disappeared.'

He made a lousy blackmailer. He was guessing. Probing. He couldn't be sure he had something.

'Goodbye, Mikka.'

Klinovec took his bottle and turned to leave.

'Aren't we going to share that?' Mikka asked, stabbing at the wrapped bottle. 'I've more to say.'

He followed Klinovec out of the liquor store and into a fruit-and-vegetable shop, where he joined a queue. A large consignment of green bananas from Cuba had caught Klinovec's eye.

Just how bad at blackmail could a low-life be? Mikka had already revealed to his victim the source and extent of his information. All Klinovec needed to establish was whether or not the man had had an accomplice, and whether or not he had a record of his findings in safe-keeping.

Mikka pocked at the fruit on display, while Klinovec stood in the queue with his bunch of green bananas. In spite of the dirty adventures of which Klinovec was master, he had never killed a man. His grubby little friend, Mikka, was about to change that.

'Where are you staying?' Klinovec asked.

'The Rossija. Do you want to go there?'

3

Lockwood ran the Iberian Desk. His shiny black hair had been confidently painted on his head with two strokes of a large pasting brush. Strangely, the look seemed to banish any doubt he had in his own abilities. He was consistent in all he undertook. Hinkley had served under him since his move from Berlin. Lockwood liked Hinkley. He confided in him. He was drawn to those who were indifferent to the invidious intimacy he himself injected into conversation. He was quick to tell the lovely Jack about the new man in Banking Section: the one with the butter curls.

'He lives in the most abominable flat, though, somewhere in Bermondsey. He smells of biscuits and vinegar, the dear.'

'Cut the crap, Lockwood. Can I go back to Barcelona?'

'Come and have tea.'

'I've had all the tea I can drink. You haven't answered my question.'

'No, you can't. Now come upstairs.'

The canteen was at the top of the building. They shared a lift with Pickering, C's deputy.

'Dull, this place,' said Lockwood to Hinkley – but for Pickering's benefit. The inference was that morale was low.

'Decent curtains wouldn't go amiss. And what about some flowers?'

Lockwood was referring to the weighted gauze curtains that screened the windows of the lower eight floors and were supposed to prevent the spray of glass splinters in the event of a bomb-blast. He had complained to Hinkley about the curtains before, but the flower-arranging . . . that was new.

'How often has continuity been emphasised, eh Jack? The thirteenth-century Cistercians were the first to plant our artificial flower-meads, and *they're* still with us, the dear boys.'

Hinkley, too, took advantage of Pickering's presence.

'Why can't I go to Barcelona?'

Lockwood pouted disapprovingly. Hinkley was out of order. Nothing more was said until they had stepped out of the lift.

'Pickering doesn't like you,' Lockwood said when Pickering was out of earshot. He opened his eyes to the full. It was a reprimand of sorts. It was also a caution. 'You do know that, don't you? He told me he thought you were "unhappy with us",' Lockwood said, mimicking Pickering. 'It was bloody obvious he was fishing. He wanted to know what I thought of you. Bloody late in asking . . . .'

'What else did he say?' Hinkley enquired blandly.

'I said: "Where do you want to put him?" He pretended to give it some thought, then he said: "He's the sort of chap who would do well in Special Branch."'

'A *policeman*?' I said.

'"The Irish Squad, perhaps," he said. "He *is* from Liverpool, isn't he?"' Lockwood pouted again. 'Vicious!'

'Do you think he might have told you this, knowing that you would tell me?' Hinkley asked glibly.

Lockwood pooh-poohed this suggestion.

'I'm not indiscreet, Jack. *I* never ask why.' They entered the canteen.'Pickering's a bit irate at the moment, you see,' continued Lockwood. 'He's having to play shuttle-diplomat with a pal. MI5 has been complaining to the Permanent Secretary. They're saying we're falling down on the job, that we haven't been able to give them intelligence of any worth on our Middle Eastern friends. They're panicking. They have C13 on full alert. They've supplemented it with detectives from CID. They have the entire Special Branch on duty. It's bloody obvious they've been caught with their pants down, too. Pickering's been round in Curzon Street simpering in front of his opposite number. Very cosy, they are. They have regular meetings. They sit in the back seat of a car with their newspapers like taxi-drivers in Battersea Park.'

'What's on our desk?' Hinkley asked.

'Three thugs went missing in Tangiers. They'd come from Damascus. They've turned up on our patch.'

'Barcelona?'

'Lisbon. Coming north. Paris or London, we think.'

'Are they carrying?'

'Clean as a whistle. There was talk of intercepting them anyway, but this trio is new. We want to see who's meeting them.'

'What's happening in Barcelona?'

'My dear boy, if you think I'm hiding anything from you, you are mistaken.'

Lockwood's attention was momentarily drawn to another quarter.

'There he goes,' he said with a benevolent sigh – it was really quite theatrical – 'our practical Christian.'

Lockwood was watching C pass along by the far wall of the canteen, his attention apparently absorbed in the cup of tea, and two Arrowroot biscuits caught in the saucer, which he carried with great care. C liked to be seen in the canteen, although he would drink his tea in the privacy of his own office.

'This latest terrorist alert doesn't seem to worry the old man unduly,' Lockwood continued.

'He's ill?' asked Hinkley, seeking confirmation. He couldn't help noticing how grey the old man appeared.

'Yes, he's been ill for some time. That doesn't seem to bother him either. He's never been one of the "hearties". Not like Pickering. If Pickering succeeds him, he'll have us all in camp playing hockey and clambering over the primrose-covered turf banks every other weekend.'

They selected a corner table away from the door.

'How is Mary?' Lockwood asked, lifting the lid of the teapot and looking inside.

'Mary is fine,' Hinkley replied, somewhat impatiently. 'And Vanessa too,' he added quickly.

'I must say,' Lockwood continued, having selected a biscuit, 'the sun *does* agree with you.'

'More crap, Lockwood. Who's temporary Head of Station?'

'Jeffers . . . from Madrid.'

'Jeffers,' repeated Hinkley sourly. 'And Snitkina? Is he still in the city?'

'You *are* anxious to get back there, aren't you? Comrade Snitkina has finished his little sweep on our patch. Six more on the plane back to Moscow. There'll be a few more faces for you when you return. Comrade Snitkina has packed his bags and is bound for Amsterdam.'

'You got a report from Barcelona on the hijacking? I left instructions with Davis.'

'The Foreign Office has been hounding us over the hijacking. They're insisting we told the Spaniards to go in guns blazing.'

'Did we?'

'We advised them, and the advice was to storm the plane. A different emphasis, you will agree. C has had a meeting with the PM. I had to write the report he submitted. You weren't any help, Jack. What the hell were you doing over there?'

'We went to the airport as unofficial observers. We took no part in it.'

'I should think not!'

'There was some confusion as to how many terrorists there were. At one point it was thought one had got off the jet with the survivors. Like everyone else, we went looking. We met the Foreign Office in the car park. It turned out there was no fourth man, but the Foreign Office isn't satisfied. They think we've got something to hide. Are you surprised?'

'It isn't over yet,' Lockwood said, sipping his tea. 'It will be the first item on the agenda for the emergency debate. There was a lot of running for cover under the cannot-be-disclosed umbrella at the TREVI meeting.' Lockwood paused to drink more tea. He took his time over the next question. 'What *really* happened to Larch? I examined the report from Davis. He's saying it was a mugging.'

'A mugging?'

'You dispute that?'

'I just wonder how he can be so sure.'

'He isn't sure, but he's saying in the absence of another reasonable explanation . . . he's saying it was a separate incident.'

'It was . . . .'

So C had settled for a simple case of mugging, thought Hinkley, *and has briefed Davis and Higgins accordingly.* The police had found no evidence to prove otherwise.

'He was on his way home?' Lockwood asked.

'I don't know,' Hinkley replied.

'He should have been in the office, shouldn't he? It *was* him, after all, who put the call through to the duty officer in London.'

'Yes, it was. He should have been in the office. He should have waited.'

'Yes. He should have waited. He wasn't killed in the office. I had it checked. It's a mystery, isn't it?'

Lockwood drank more tea. Hinkley had difficulty swallowing his. He ate a biscuit instead.

'Anyway,' said Lockwood, pretending to be cheerful again, 'Davis's report went to Pickering, and I used Davis's version of events in the report C submitted to the PM.'

He paused, as though he expected Hinkley to comment.

'Right,' said Hinkley belatedly.

'You see, I didn't call you in for debriefing because Pickering told me you've had a word with C.'

'Yes. That's right.'

'But I thought you should know . . . the official story, that is.'

'Right.'

Lockwood's attempt at eliciting information was unsuccessful. Hinkley was giving nothing away.

Now it was Hinkley's attention that was drawn to another quarter. Barbara deWitt had entered the canteen with a heavy-set man who was regaling her with some anecdote. The visitor now has his back to Hinkley and Lockwood, but Hinkley recognised him: the crew-cut; the head shaped like a bucket. It was his American friend from the Berlin days, Otis. Otis Baxter. He was a little fatter than he had been in the Hamburg nightclub photographs Hinkley had helped to set up. That aside, Otis Baxter's appearance was unaltered.

'Oh not *him*,' said Lockwood. 'Oh Christ, he's seen us. He's coming over. What *is* he like. Look at that shirt and tie. He's dressed like a bookie's runner. Hello, Mister Baxter.'

Lockwood rose to his feet and extended his hand.

'Hello, Mister Lockwood,' boomed Baxter, vigorously shaking the hand. He got a kick out of the formal address. 'And hello to you, too, Jack Hinkley! Good God, Jack, it's been a while.'

Hinkley greeted Baxter warmly. He was genuinely pleased to see the man. He concluded his greeting with: 'Lockwood says you're dressed like a bookie's runner.'

Lockwood didn't bat an eyelid.

'Pretty sharply dressed yourselves,' Baxter replied with a generous smile. 'You're as neat as ever I seen you,' he said to Hinkley. 'I bet you still got your money rolled, dirty notes on the outside.'

He insisted Hinkley take his money out, to show how much of a buddy Jack was.

'There, you see!'

'Won't you join us?' Hinkley asked.

'No, I'm over there with Barbara.'

'A social call?' enquired Lockwood spitefully.

'No. I'm here on official business. But I have to say I noticed Barbara's body has that Grecian bend, you know . . . .' Baxter arched his back.

Lockwood was disgusted.

Hinkley knew to expect just such a comment from Otis Baxter.

'She's as pale as a peeled banana, though,' Baxter continued. He pointed to Hinkley with his thumb. 'He's all right, but the rest of you guys should get youselves a sunlamp in here, or you'll end up like Chalkie.'

The 'Chalkie' reference to C didn't go down well with Lockwood. It was a cheap remark about a sick man.

'Barbara looks anxious,' Lockwood said to Baxter curtly.

'Oh, right. See you guys.'

Baxter left their table.

'No,' concluded Lockwood venomously in his wake, 'Barbara doesn't look anxious. She looks apprehensive.'

Baxter returned.

'You going to be around?' he asked Hinkley.

'A few days, no more.'

'I'll give you a call. Same Chelsea number, right?'

'Same number.'

'What is he doing here?' Hinkley asked when Baxter had taken his seat at Barbara deWitt's table.

'Oh, he's scrounging. What else?'

'Last I heard of him, he was working out of their warehouse in Washington.'

97

'The warehouse boy was promoted. Presumably they felt he had social skills,' Lockwood commented witheringly.

'What do they want?'

'Our cousins are looking for whatever we have on Snitkina. Barbara and I have had to deal with him. Barbara's been in Kew much of the time. It's been left to me. It's been a tough week. Look at him! Now he's trying to get into Barbara's knickers as well as her computer. It really is disgusting. We shouldn't allow the Americans in here. We should arrange to meet them in coffee-bars.'

'So he's now based in London?'

'Unfortunately, he is.'

Lockwood and Hinkley parted company in the corridor outside the canteen, Lockwood to his desk, Hinkley to Pickering's office. Hinkley was determined to discover how long he was to be kept in suspense.

Pickering refused to see him. He sent a message that he was to go home and wait for a call.

Hinkley collected the parcel containing Davis's shoes, and left the building. He decided to walk back to Chelsea. He needed the air. He crossed Westminster Bridge with his new coat buttoned to the collar and the parcel tightly tucked under his arm. He wasn't surprised to see extra policemen on duty at the Houses of Parliament. In London and in other population centres throughout Britain, the anti-terrorist squad remained on full alert. It had been supplemented by a large contingent of detectives and Special Branch officers. There was still no trace of the third suitcase bomb. The attacks expected on the heels of the Paris bombing were slow in coming.

★

The TREVI meeting chaired by the Home Secretary concerned itself primarily with practical measures to counter terrorist attacks throughout Europe. There were the usual calls for increased airport and on-board security. Inevitably, Belfast's Aldergrove Airport was held up as a model of the former, El-Al of the latter.

Now, for the first time, proposals for the use of the SAS and German G9 forces in consort with other counter-terrorist groups were openly discussed. Not only was there support for action of a preemptive nature, but there was also support – albeit from a minority – for covert operations against terrorist bases outside Europe. Again, the Israelis were referred to, the activities of their MOSSAD cited as an example.

The Paris bombing was discussed. Where was the third suitcase bomb now? Could the combined security forces of Europe not find one suitcase? Seemingly not.

The Barcelona hijacking was discussed. There was criticism of the Spaniards' handling of the affair. Had they been too hasty? The Spanish delegate reiterated his government's insistence that they had properly discharged their duty to protect citizens in accordance with the EEC directive that promoted a firm response to international terrorism. Furthermore, he added, it was British intelligence in London who had put a compelling case for storming the jet immediately it landed.

The Home Secretary, in his capacity as chairman, cautioned against the assumption that one worked on the premise that casualties were inevitable and that there was an acceptable casualty rate. This said, the TREVI committee officially sanctioned limited preemptive action in Europe. A press statement was issued. No press conference was given.

At the crisis meeting of EEC Interior Ministers, the Spanish Interior Minister was subjected to harsher criticism. Again, the Spanish invoked the EEC directive on terrorism. Had not all member-states agreed to meet the threat with firmness? Yes, it was agreed, but no one was in the business of simply teaching terrorists a lesson. The object was to save lives, to use force only as a last resort. The firmness referred to entailed the tightening of security at air and sea ports, the tightening of visa control for certain non-EEC countries, and a resolve to defeat the terrorist by committing increased resources to intelligence-gathering activities. Again, the Spanish drew attention to the involvement of British Intelligence in the decision to storm the hijacked jet at Barcelona Airport.

The British Interior Minister had no comment to make, other than to say that British security services would offer their EEC colleagues advice in good faith if advice was sought.

The minutes of the TREVI meeting were assessed. It was unanimously agreed that there was an urgent need to improve security measures at all air and sea ports, and that visa control for certain non-EEC countries should be reviewed. There was disagreement over preemptive action. However, no Minister present was prepared to rule out completely the sanctioning of all clandestine operations. They each knew that such operations had been undertaken in the past, and would continue, regardless of political edict. Even the British Defence Intelligence Committee, charged with the task of monitoring operations that had political ramifications, at times found itself confined to compiling retrospective reports in the absence of prior knowledge of the operations. For the politicians, it was a question of whether or not the government admitted that such tactics were employed. For the British Interior Minister, the position was clear. The service he would not refer to by name – let alone discuss its activities – was free from public accountability.

A motion to endorse the TREVI committee's decision to officially sanction limited preemptive action in Europe was carried.

In his apartment in Moscow, Klinovec lay on his bed watching the flashes on the ceiling caused by trolley buses hitting the junction in the electric wires down in the street. He slipped into his pocket a small unused and unregistered pistol he had kept hidden. This time he would have a car when he met Mikka, the blackmailer. He would need it for the body.

He had arranged to meet Mikka at night at the Stadium for Young Pioneers. At their business meeting in the Rossija Hotel, he had been able to establish that Mikka was working alone. However, he had been unable to discover whether or not the man had a record of his findings in safe-keeping. Klinovec was prepared to take a chance on there being no record. He had no alternative.

Mikka naively thought that because the stadium was in a busy, brightly lit part of the city, he was safe.

Klinovec shot him once in his stupid head as soon as he got into the car.

Two hours later, with the little blackmailer safely in the sewers, Klinovec was helping with a second removal in spite of a sore leg and muscles, which had been sapped of their energy. A neighbour had asked him to help carry a large television set down six flights of stairs. To Klinovec it seemed to weigh as much as the corpse.

Klinovec led the way down the stairs. His neighbour explained that he was buying a colour set. He had sold this black-and-white set to his brother-in-law. He hurried Klinovec down the stairs as quickly as he dared. He had a taxi waiting.

4

Again, in Peter Jones's department store in Chelsea, Hinkley searched for a wedding present. He hadn't searched properly on his last visit. He had felt that he should return. Mary had already bought a present that would be from both of them, but he wanted to give his daughter something extra, something *he* had chosen. It was proving difficult.

Eventually, he made his purchase. He arranged for it to be delivered. He returned to the house. The house was quiet now. There was no tuneless whistle, no rustic prattle. Geoffrey had returned to his farm in Cheshire to make arrangements for his extended visit in the south that would include Vanessa's wedding and his cancer operation.

Mary and Vanessa had not yet returned. Hinkley rewound and played the telephone answering-machine. There had been one call. No message left.

He went upstairs, put Davis's shoes in his suitcase and moved the suitcase back into the spare bedroom. In light of their torpid behaviour in bed the previous night, he thought it best that he and Mary sleep apart. That way there was less confusion. The obscure path he trod was safer with clear margins. He would rest in a bed without Mary. He would wait patiently for the telephone call that would restore his job.

The telephone rang.

It was Otis Baxter.

Baxter invited Hinkley out to dinner. He nominated a Thai restaurant on Fulham Road. Hinkley agreed to it. There was no invitation for Mary.

'Just you and me,' Baxter said.

Hinkley left a note for Mary. He said it was business. He promised not to be late.

'So, you like Barbara deWitt?' Hinkley asked, reclining on a couch in the restaurant.

'Sure I like her,' replied Baxter, 'but she's not much fun.'

'Barbara deWitt is possibly the brightest person in the building. I don't see her falling for your frontier charm, Otis. Did you get the information you wanted?'

'I don't know, do I? It depends on how much you guys are keeping to yourselves.'

Baxter regarded the petite waitress and the starters with equal relish.

'How's your wife?' he asked distractedly.

'Mary is well.'

'You two must come round to my place for dinner.'

'Where do they keep you?'

'I've got a small place in Blackheath. It's a converted coach-house. The handles and locks are too close to the door-frames, and the lid on the john won't stand up, but it's comfortable. I've got a rock star living next door. It's quiet most of the time. He's never there. How long did you say you'd be in London, Jack?'

'A few days. My daughter is getting married.'

'You got a picture of her to show me?'

'Do you know anybody in our business who carries a family photograph?'

'Right,' Baxter said, nodding to himself. 'Well maybe you'll bring her to dinner, too.'

For the first time since arriving in London, Hinkley felt at ease. In spite of the fact that he had in the past compromised Baxter. Had the situation been reversed Baxter would have done the same to him. Perhaps he could show Baxter the photographs some day.

The easiness lingered when convivial conversation again gave way to shop-talk.

'What's your interest in Snitkina?' Hinkley asked, knowing he would not be given a full and honest answer.

'The same as yours,' replied Baxter. 'We don't want him disturbing our people. We don't want him making extra work for us. He's making a name for himself in Moscow reassessing personnel in every goddamn KGB station in Western Europe. He wants a big ship named after him. Maybe we can trip him up, dirty him a little. You were watching him in Barcelona, weren't you?'

'We knew he was there,' replied Hinkley guardedly.

'Then that damn hijacking happened . . . .' Baxter, resting on his side, chewed rapidly, swallowed, made an appreciative noise. 'That fourth-man story in the press. Garbage, right?'

'At one point the Spanish thought they had let one get away, but they soon realised there had only been three of them. Passengers and crew confirmed that, but the rumour persisted.'

'It's just that our boys picked up on that story, too. When they put the survivors on flights home, they were one passenger short. They figure he just took a train or a bus out of there without telling anybody.'

'Is that what your people think?'

'Sure. Why not? The guy was in a big hurry.'

More food arrived. Hinkley had been unadventurous. He had ordered a lightly spiced meal. Baxter had ordered hot dishes. He liked to burn. He liked to suck in air to fan the flames. Again, he chewed rapidly and swallowed.

'Isn't this wonderful?' He inhaled.

'Very nice.' Hinkley wasn't in the mood for anything exotic.

'He's gone now, of course,' said Baxter cryptically.

'Who's gone where?' The food *did* taste good.

'Snitkina. To Amsterdam.'

'Otis, you've got all the information you're going to get. You got it from Barbara deWitt. I've nothing more for you.'

'Okay, Jack. You know me. Always looking for more. There are hunters and gatherers: you know that, Jack. I'm a hunter. Always have been. Fishing, shooting, even rustling.'

'Rustling?' Hinkley scoffed. 'I thought that was confined to the Wild West.'

'Wild, my ass. Rustling takes patience. You've got to be prepared to wait. You pick out your ranch. You pick out your herd. You pick out your animal. It takes being gentle. You got to walk your animal as near to that damn truck as you can get it. Come on, Henry. Over here, Henry. Over by the truck, Henry. As near to that damn truck as you can get it. *Then* you shoot it in the head with your gun.'

'I thought you rounded up the entire herd, took it to some box canyon or other, and changed the brand on each hide,' said Hinkley, making a pantomime of being impressed.

'Are you kidding? What the hell would I do with a herd of cattle? No-no. This is where you get your chainsaw out and you cut him up on the spot. The steam is still rising off the guts when you're forty miles down the road. You can fill a couple of freezers with one carcass.'

Baxter had a large repertoire of such stories. He liked to play the buffoon. That was his first line of defence: the outer skin of his cover. Being a loud American was the ill-fitting suit he wore. It was a testament to its effectiveness that one couldn't imagine Otis Baxter in anything else.

Hinkley did not encourage him further with a reply.

'It doesn't have to be in America. Any old field with a cow in it. Now you, Jack: you're a gatherer. You go round picking up your nuts and your berries . . . .'

'Otis, what is this leading to?'

'You're a useful guy to know, Jack. You get to know the lie of the land: where the cows are; when the farmer is out. You hear what I'm saying?'

'Is this one of those explanatory anecdotes they dish up to you at Langley? Is this what they tell you to say?'

'Jack, I swear to God, I'm sick of steak.'

'Bollocks. What are you saying?'

Baxter kept smiling agreeably.

'We've had Snitkina's apartment in Barcelona wired since he moved in. He's not so thorough when it comes to weeding out spook gadgets. We know he had a visitor the night of the hijacking. We think it was Josef Klinovec. One of your guys was killed that night. He was watching Klinovec, wasn't he? Klinovec was the missing passenger – the fourth man – right?' Baxter was still smiling but the sense of ease in the room had suddenly evaporated.

Hinkley made no reply.

'Is that why Chalkie has you back here? You called the panic desk in London, they told you to pick up Klinovec, and you botched it? I need to know, Jack. We're on to something hot in Paris. We think we know who he was going to see. You can share in it. It would be a chance to redeem yourself.'

In Baxter's cheap proposition, there was plenty to worry Hinkley, and nothing from which to benefit.

Hinkley said nothing. He carried on eating his spiced food until it was all gone.

'Look, Jack, I'm sorry. I don't mean to be pushy. I know I'm out of order. Just forget it, OK?'

'I've to wear a morning-suit to this wedding,' said Hinkley wistfully.

Hinkley went home to wait. Mary was in the basement flat with Vanessa and the dress-maker. They were making final alterations to the wedding dress. Hinkley thought he might be shocked when he saw his daughter in her wedding dress for the first time, but he wasn't. Instead, the scene prompted a sense of relief. Vanessa was looking out for herself, doing what she wanted to do. She didn't care about his not liking her future husband. He admired her for that.

'It's beautiful,' he said, and stepped forward to kiss her on the cheek.

She was pleased he approved. She immediately returned his gesture.

There were reciprocal gestures of respect made between Jack and Mary, too. She was not going to ask about his evening out. She was not going to mention his moving out of her bedroom. He hadn't asked her about the Peter who was looking for her. He hadn't even asked about her ceasing to smoke. Now they were both trying to make it easy for each other.

'Remember, Jack, you've to go to the dress-hire firm in the morning,' said Mary.

'I haven't forgotten,' he replied.

5

Hinkley felt good in the morning-suit. He wouldn't have to say much at the wedding reception. It was easier for him to be reserved when he was wearing formal dress.

'Well?' Mary asked, when she was finally ready. She lifted her hands from her body and turned. 'What I used to call "shocking pink", our daughter calls "cerise".'

'It's lovely, Mary,' said Hinkley. 'Truly lovely.'

She was happy in the bold colour. Content, because her daughter had asked her to wear that dress.

'I haven't decided which shoes,' she said. She crossed the floor, raised on the balls of her feet. She had been wearing high heels so long, the ligaments above her heels had shortened. 'These, perhaps?' She picked up a pair of shoes.

'What about those?' asked Hinkley, pointing to another pair.

'Darling, I *can't* wear those. Anything with a heel smaller than a postage stamp marks polished floors. They might have a parquet floor.'

Why didn't she admit she just didn't want to wear them?

In these circles it was unusual for the bride's family not to host the wedding celebrations, but such were the couple's wishes. It was decidedly odd to be going to a house of strangers, to stand on their polished floor and be welcomed as family. Jack and Mary were nervous. Jack had telephoned Paul to offer him a lift, but there was no answer. He had also left the Kent number, the hotel number, and travel arrangements, with Lockwood.

They lost their way looking for the hotel. They were late. Mary was distraught.

'They won't have started yet,' Hinkley said, idiotically.

'Of course they won't,' cried Mary, '*you're* giving her away. That's not the point. Oh God. You should have let me drive. We're late for our own daughter's wedding.'

When they found the hotel, Hinkley rang the family house to announce their arrival. They dumped their overnight case with the porter and drove at speed to the church.

'You should be with her now, Jack. You should have been with her an hour ago. We should have come down early this morning, as they suggested ... but no ....'

'It's all right. I've arranged to meet Vanessa at the church door.'

'You've "arranged ...",' Mary complained bitterly. Ever the professional, Jack.'

★

Hinkley parked illegally.

Mary ran skilfully in her high heels to the church door, and abandoned her husband there. She pushed her shoulder-pads back into place and took the aisle with remarkable grace. She joined her brother, Geoffrey, who, until that moment, was the chief member of the bride's party present.

There was no sign of Jack's brother, Paul.

★

At the lavish wedding reception in the house, inclement weather forced the guests to stay indoors. Hinkley remained doggedly professional by being reserved. Mary did most of the polite talking. Nothing Hinkley saw endeared Roger to him, but Vanessa was happy. At least there was that to celebrate.

Posing with his family for photographs, some of which were taken in front of a tapestry hung in the hallway of the manor, Hinkley felt no further from his daughter, no closer to his wife, but more respectful of both. As a family, they had fared better than many families to which their friends belonged. However, Hinkley's wish to be free of the spectre of his own professional demise on that day was not granted. In the small parish church on the edge of Canterbury, he had given his daughter to be married. In Barcelona, his cat was on the balcony of his vacant apartment, its front paws running on the window-pane. In Moscow, Klinovec was celebrating another secret triumph.

The abandoned cat, the smug Czech, the circumvented spy, had returned from a run in the gutters. For all of them, the waiting between forays was nothing new. They were creatures who had learnt to wait in spite of hunger, but of the three Hinkley had fared worst. The cat had a window at which to wait. It had the option of scavenging. The

Czech would return to his normal duties as Deputy Head of Directorate S. He could, if threatened, find enemies of the state among those who posed a threat. Hinkley was suspended, under investigation, without representation. Davis and Higgins would say what they had been told to say. Lockwood would stand by him, that was true. Lockwood would not allow them to pursue allegations of incompetence without there being a proper inquiry, which he would chair. C would ensure that the Iberian Desk cleared Hinkley. If Lockwood didn't already know it, C would ensure that he learnt of Klinovec's true status.

In Barcelona, Hinkley had made a proper evaluation, given the information available to him at the time. How could the charge be one of incompetence? It was conceivable that C was the only other person to know Klinovec's true status. The obvious conclusion to draw was that Hinkley was to be used as a scapegoat – but what were they waiting for? Why had they not just fired him; sent him to the Irish Squad with mediocre references? The whole hijacking business was already old news. There was now the threat of a wave of terrorist bombings throughout Europe.

Hinkley, Mary and her brother were among the last guests to leave the house. It was after 1 AM when they left for their respective hotels. Geoffrey had been put in a hotel not far from the house. Hinkley and his wife had further to travel. Theirs had started as a pub and had recently become a hotel, with extensions to the rear and side. When they returned, they found it was shut tight. There were no night staff on duty, which was most unusual, not to say, unacceptable, but then the couple had left for the church in such a hurry that they had made no provision for returning late. They had not been given a key, nor had they been told which room they were to occupy. Presumably, unless prior arrangements were made, the owner/manager kept to a midnight or 1 AM curfew.

Mary rang the doorbell repeatedly. There was no reply.

They went round to the back of the building. The back door was locked. Hinkley pressed the service bell. No reply.

A kitchen window had been left open.

'I don't think you should,' said Mary. It was cold. She was beginning to shiver.

'It's their fault. They should have given us a key.'

Hinkley got in through the kitchen window and admitted Mary. He pressed a light-switch, and the fluorescents flickered on.

The door between the kitchen and the rest of the hotel was locked.

'What will we do now?' Mary asked. She was still shivering.

'I'll think of something.'

The harsh light reflected in the white and steel was uncomfortable. They were both exhausted. They were also hungry. It had been a long time since the wedding breakfast, and they had refused subsequent offers of food. Hinkley looked in the large fridge.

'I don't think you should,' repeated Mary, and yawned.

'It's the least they can do for us,' said Hinkley.

In London, at Baxter's Blackheath mews, there were others carefully rummaging. They had been there before, and had found nothing. They found nothing this time either, but they would be back.

'This is ridiculous,' Mary said, with her nervous little laugh. Hinkley had made her a plate of sandwiches. Turkey with parsley. Ham with mustard. Cheese with pickle. He had sharpened the knife to cut the turkey. It was a not-entirely-unfamiliar seduction scene. For a moment, they were back at Oxford, Jack knowing no better than to attempt to force-feed the anorexic undergraduate.

'Agreed,' said Hinkley.

'Seriously, what are we going to do?'

Hinkley quartered the sandwiches, then said: 'We'll try the bell once more. If no one answers, we'll go to your brother's hotel. If necessary, we'll sleep on his floor. I'm not driving back to London without sleep.'

'All right. But what about our bag?'

'I'll call here first thing in the morning.'

It seemed a reasonable suggestion.

'Bloody idiots not giving us a key,' said Hinkley, eating his first sandwich-quarter. 'What sort of hotel is it that doesn't have a night-porter?'

'It's an inn, darling. You can't expect . . . .'

'Just eat your sandwich, will you?' he interrupted.

Mary ate a sandwich for Jack.

Their eyes had got used to the light by now.

'What are you staring at?' Mary asked sportively.

Hinkley wanted her body – that scrawny body in pink – but more than that, he wanted to confide in her.

'Have another sandwich, Mary.'

'I haven't finished this one yet.'

They tried the front doorbell again. No reply.

When they got to the other hotel, they found Geoffrey and several other wedding guests having a tea party in a corner of the partially lit lounge. It was a merry gathering. Geoffrey had made new friends. He was delighted to see his sister and brother-in-law again, in spite of having parted company from them less than two hours earlier. He invited them to share in the tea and biscuits.

'No thanks, Geoff,' said Hinkley, 'we've just had something.'

Mary went on to explain their predicament.

Hinkley asked the night-porter – the bearer of tea and biscuits – if there was a vacant room to be had.

There was, he said.

Hinkley signed the register.

'"Mr and Mrs Hinkley",' read the night-porter. 'That *is* remarkable. We've had a reservation in that name for tonight.' He pointedly referred to the reservation sheet. 'There, you see. Can I take it you are the party in question?' he asked officiously. 'Just for the record, sir . . . you understand.'

'Yes, you may.'

In London, at Hinkley's Chelsea house, others had been where they shouldn't have been – but with a purpose. They, too, had found nothing. They, too, would be back.

'No luggage, sir?' the porter asked, rising on his feet in order to look over the desk.

'No luggage,' replied Hinkley flatly. The White Swan Inn should have been the White House Hotel.

That night, Jack and Mary made a desperate sort of love. It was as if, inexplicably, both felt that time was running out. They both attempted to conceal that desperation, each from the other.

6

The lake was everything. It made her hair float, her cuts crimson. It was to the lake she would bring her lover before taking him to her bed. The sky above it, the trees about it, the stream that fed it: they were all part of it. Light from the sky, wind through the trees, fresh water by the stream: they kept it alive. He would love it as she did. She feared the squalor of cities. It would keep her from the lake. It would trap her spirit. If she lived in a city, she would be forever reaching for the sky through the bars of a drain. Her lover would have to stay with her in the house by the lake. It was the only place she could be happy. She'd wear make-up for him. She'd dress in evening gowns to go out, but she'd have to wear flat shoes. High heels would break on the rough path to the lake.

That was the teenage Mary. So Geoffrey told Jack. They weren't his words. They were Mary's. She confided in her brother. Geoffrey recounted this to his brother-in-law in the quiet of the Cheshire home after the funeral of his wife, May. It was his way of saying: look after Mary; you are the only other person she trusts.

Mary had managed at Oxford. Oxford was clean. Exclusive. She could go home most weekends. Coming to London with Jack was an act of faith. It was arduous at first. He wasn't earning much. She was reluctant to work, because work kept her in London. She still went home at weekends. Often she would stay for a week or more. Much later, when they were living in Chelsea, she stopped running and hiding. Jack, the child, the house: they made her feel more secure, but they also left her increasingly introspective.

Now, she was running again. Back to Cheshire. To the lake. Jack had never seen the lake. It must have been some distance from the house. Perhaps it was only in Mary's imagination.

In the car on the way back to London, Hinkley was still in his morning-suit, but Mary was wearing a cotton skirt with brightly coloured sights of Rome printed on it. She had changed into it in the car outside the White Swan Hotel after Hinkley had had a disagreement with the hotel management as to whether or not there was a bill to be paid. Mary had changed into the clothes she liked to wear when returning to the house in Cheshire: the clothes her husband imagined she wore on weekend trips out of London with her lover. Now that they had been together, his resolve not to interfere in her life was crumbling. It was enough that his daughter had married an idler. He couldn't bear the thought of someone taking advantage of Mary. His concern for her was genuine, but it was tempered with jealousy. The pressures on him seemed to have doubled overnight. Their spent passion made him panic. He needed to get back to the cruel, physical, short-lived affairs with dark women in Barcelona: back to Pilar; back to flirting with Xavier's wife; back to his grubby work.

Part Three

1

In London, in Otis Baxter's mews in Blackheath, Hinkley and Baxter had an impromptu bottle party.

'Lockwood told me you keep a fancy woman in Barcelona,' said Baxter.

'No he didn't,' replied Hinkley.

They were both slightly drunk.

'His words,' insisted Baxter. 'Fancy woman.'

'Aside from his not telling you, Otis, it isn't true,' replied Hinkley, stiffly.

'I figured he was leading me on. The guy needs a vacation. You take this Snitkina business. He got all upset when I asked him a couple of questions about him. He was like some damn art cop blowin' his whistle.'

'Lockwood's a good man; good at his job,' said Hinkley morosely.

'Pickering should make him take a vacation.'

'Pickering,' scoffed Hinkley.

Pickering was again in Curzon Street, in consultations with colleagues at MI5. MI5 made no more complaints to the Permanent Secretary. Pickering had something new for them on the movements and intentions of three Middle

Eastern–based terrorist cells planning attacks in Britain – intelligence which, if accurate, was remarkably comprehensive. Pickering wasn't in a position to reveal the source, because even he had been denied this information.

★

Throughout the continent of Europe, anti-terrorist squads remained on alert. The search for the third suitcase bomb continued. So, too, in Britain, but now the additional men and women drafted from CID and Special Branch could be returned to normal duties. A plan to take preemptive action in accordance with the TREVI decision was about to be drawn up.

On the eighth floor of the eight-storey headquarters of the KGB in Dzerzhinsky Square, the Director was hearing circumstantial evidence against Major Josef Klinovec, Deputy Head of Directorate S of the First Chief Directorate. As yet, the Director was far from convinced that there was a case for Comrade Klinovec to answer. Klinovec had proved himself to be a tireless and ingenious defender of the State. If anything, the Director would have been more prepared to hear a case brought against Klinovec's immediate superior, Vigodskaya, whose performance was disappointing. Certainly, no charge of treason had been made against Klinovec. Attention had been drawn to a number of irregularities – that was all. In certain matters, the Deputy Head of Directorate S could make his report directly to the Director's office, thus creating apparent discrepancies or gaps in reports. The Director was confident that Klinovec would be able to fully answer the questions that were to be put to him.

★

In another part of Moscow, in an apartment block reserved for foreigners, the residents were having problems with the plumbing. Resident foreigners were usually last to complain to the authorities about the all-too-familiar maintenance problems that beset Soviet life, rural and urban. This was one of the better apartment blocks. Unlike many, shortcuts to meet construction deadlines had not been taken. The plumbing should have been sound, but there was some flooding on the ground floor, and a foul smell was rising from the drain beside the militiaman's cardboard hut at the entrance. Underneath the foundations of the building, the sewage trap that led to the main pipe had been partially blocked by a body, but the rats had set to work. In time, sewage from the apartment building would flow unimpeded through the ribcage of the deceased.

In Amsterdam, Snitkina was waiting to hear from an agent in London before returning to Moscow to prosecute his case.

In an apartment building in Barcelona, Davis and Higgins were searching Hinkley's rooms, carefully going through all his belongings. The cat had left them to it. It was now KGB goons who were looking through the balcony window. They were watching from the fire-escape on the building opposite.

In the office on the Paslo de Colón, Jeffers, temporary Head of Station, had settled in nicely. The premises had been declared sterile. He personally had discarded the ailing potted plants. He had had Davis and Higgins out photographing the new KGB contingent sent to replace those Snitkina had relieved of their duty. While Davis and Higgins were in Hinkley's apartment, Jeffers was studying the coroner's report on Larch's death, which had only now been delivered to the British Consulate. The inquest had been a protracted affair.

Furthermore, the Foreign Office was still badgering MI6 about Larch's activities on the night of his murder. Jeffers was compiling another report that would confirm the smuggling story.

Back in London, Lord Peacher came out of a second meeting with the Prime Minister bitterly disappointed. Having again expressed a personal sympathy with the bereaved, the Prime Minister had stood by Century House. Advice had been given in good faith, the Prime Minister concluded.

In Harley Street, C was visiting his new doctor. While the doctor examined him, he reviewed his decision to brief MI5 on the terrorist activities planned in Britain. He decided that, on balance, he had made the correct decision. He needed the domestic mob off his back. He needed to make political gain. He would ensure that the Prime Minister and the Foreign Secretary credited MI6 with the successful penetration of the three terrorist cells from the Middle East.

2

Peter was a Catholic priest.

Hinkley followed his wife. She had taken the day off from teaching her Japanese businessmen to visit her brother at the Royal Marsden. Geoffrey had had his operation. There had been unexpected complications. He was very low. Mary stayed with him as long as she was allowed, then went to the priest. She called to him at the presbytery. They were indiscreet. Hinkley saw them embrace behind gauze curtains. The priest was hot for her. He was her spiritual and bodily comforter – something Hinkley, her life-long partner, had failed to be.

Hinkley went to Charing Cross to return his morning-suit. He then went looking for his brother in Soho.

He couldn't find the doorway that led to the cramped first-floor studio Paul had once brought him to, eager as he was to show off his place of work, but with no models present. Perhaps Hinkley was unable to find it because of his hangover.

Hinkley saw Soho as London's largest orphanage. Like his brother, he belonged there, in as much as any misfit belonged anywhere. Hinkley had a good eye for orphans. One of his childhood haunts was the grounds of an orphanage. His wanderings often terminated at its gates. He would climb over the wall. He didn't want to play with the children. He wanted to watch them. His mother used to threaten to send him and Paul there if they misbehaved. There wasn't much chance of playing with the children, even if he wanted to. They were strictly supervised. They weren't allowed to run. Jack could run. Faster than any of them. Faster than those who forbade the running. Furthermore, he knew intimately the passages through the undergrowth. He knew the lie of the ditch, the distance between trees, the climbable branches, the seasonal cover.

He used to watch from close quarters. He'd watch the children move like monks, fight like dogs, sit in rows, eat in silence. Probation was a way of life for Jack. His was a cold examination of what he had escaped thus far. If he was sent to the orphanage, he would not be able to fight as they did, he decided, nor would he be able to sit with his back as straight as theirs, but he would be able to keep silent. He would be able to walk like a monk until it was time to run the passage through the undergrowth by the wall and beyond. No one would be able catch him.

One sunny spring morning, when he had mitched from school and was watching his soulmates from the undergrowth, he was spotted and he bolted over the wall. He trudged home and climbed the drainpipe to his bedroom window, intending to hide out until he could show his face. That was the sunny morning he first encountered his mother in the arms of 'Uncle' Frank. He was surprised at the hairs on Frank's back, and the paleness of his mother's large breasts, and how gently she closed the door on him.

Jack knew that it wasn't right, but at the time, he wasn't disturbed by the encounter. He was aware of having learnt a big secret. He knew that he had touched a great weakness. He knew he had credit.

When Jack learnt that his father knew about the affair, he ripped the front passenger seat of the family Cortina with his penknife. His mother painstakingly repaired the car upholstery with a line of neat stitching.

Wandering Soho now, Hinkley's normally astute response to human frailty had been reduced to anger.

★

Father Peter Green was in the vestry, dressing his face in front of a small mirror. He had thinned his eyebrows with tweezers. He had oiled and combed his hair. He was a dark-featured man. He had dyed his graying hair raven black. It had taken the dye well. His face was shiny. He had recently wet-shaved. He was trimming the hair above his temples with a nail scissors when Hinkley entered. The priest was not embarrassed by his own display of vanity.

He recognised his visitor. 'Jack Hinkley!' he declared pleasantly.

'Mrs Hinkley's husband,' Hinkley countered.

Father Green chose to ignore the sarcasm in his visitor's voice. 'Come in, come in.'

'You've been screwing my wife,' Hinkley said, and walked to the mantelpiece to examine a portrait of the Pope.

Understandably, there was a pause.

'Please, Jack,' said the priest, 'this is no place for such words.'

'Isn't it? I thought you could speak your mind in church. Unburden yourself.' He turned to face the priest. 'Or do we have to get into a box for that?' Hinkley knew he was letting himself down, but he didn't care. He looked his rival up and down. 'Preen yourself in here before every show, do you? You're some sort of holy ticket tout, only when the poor bastards get inside, they find you're the entertainment as well. But you like that, don't you?'

'You misunderstand the church, and you misrepresent your wife.'

'She's told me everything,' Hinkley lied. 'Ring her.'

The darkness in Hinkley intimidated the priest. He made no move until Hinkley forced him to remove his cassock. Hinkley took hold of the garment at the neck and pulled hard. The priest was unbalanced. There was a renting of cloth. The celluloid collar fell to the tiled floor. The man was profoundly shocked by the attack. He fumbled with the torn cassock. 'Why do you humiliate me?' he asked, wetting his lips.

'Jesus!' exclaimed Hinkley. '*I* was just about to say that! Now I'll have to think of something else.'

There was a silence while Hinkley thought. It was a bizarre pause.

'To answer your question,' he continued, 'I know where you've been.'

'This is a dreadful mistake,' said the priest.

Hinkley couldn't understand the priest lying for that kind of passion. In Hinkley's world, a uniform didn't make a hypocrite of a liar. He snatched the cassock from the priest's trembling hand. 'I want this for a dressing gown. I think it's the cassock she likes. I don't have a uniform in my job.'

131

'Please,' said Father Green. 'I ask you to think about what you are doing.'

Hinkley complied with the request. It was another bizarre, short-lived interlude.

'My old man had a uniform,' he said ponderously. 'It didn't do much for him – not with my mother . . . but then, my old man was on the buses.' Hinkley walked away with the cassock.

Father Green stood in his underwear in the vestry doorway watching as Hinkley purposefully moved down the aisle and threw open one half of the large double-door. He sobbed as he knelt to pick up his collar, the little plastic cradle on the tiles. He had failed to protect Mary. That was worse than being found out.

It was not lost on Hinkley that professionally, he had much in common with the priest. The priest had attempted to carry through the deception, had kept it to a simple misunderstanding, had sewn seeds of doubt.

Hinkley dropped the priest's cassock in the river. The incident he had created appalled yet steadied him.

3

Klinovec took his time over the report he filed on the Barcelona affair. He did not commit to paper the nature of his business trip to Paris. He was not expected to do so. His network was virtually autonomous. Only the head of Klinovec's Directorate and the Director himself were privy to such information. Of the two, Klinovec was most worried about his immediate superior, Vigodskaya. If Vigodskaya were to learn that he had not simply evaded capture in Barcelona – for Vigodskaya would know from Snitkina's report that at least one British agent had followed him to Snitkina's apartment – but that he had been caught by MI6 agents and subsequently released, he would have to fall back on the contingency plan C had concocted: a plan in which he had little faith.

In fact, Vigodskaya had already closely studied Snitkina's report on the incident, and was waiting to hear more from him in Amsterdam. Snitkina in turn was still waiting for word from London.

In London, C worked late into the night. He fed his body on nicotine and tannin. His most senior agent in Moscow was out on a limb when he needed his services most. There was nothing he could do to lessen the danger, that had not already been done. They would both have to be patient. What preoccupied C was finding a cut-out for Klinovec. There was nobody in place whom Klinovec was prepared to trust with his life. Besides, from the outset it had been agreed that the operation would be run outside the MI6 network. The Americans would be kept out of it, too. There would have to be a new recruit. It would have to be Klinovec who recruited the agent. Klinovec would move with the utmost caution. It would be a long time before he approached anyone. Without the cut-out, Klinovec would have to take more risks, or cease to operate. In this matter, the seminal problem for C was measuring precisely the risk another man might take.

That same evening, Hinkley was visiting Lockwood at his home in Richmond. He was glad to be out of the Chelsea house, away from Mary. That evening, when he boarded the District Line train at Sloane Square, he was aware of being followed.

'Oh yes,' said Lockwood, looking out from behind the curtain of darkened upstairs window. 'I see him. Dressed like a football hooligan.'

'Dressed for the cold.'

'I can't say I recognise him. You sure he's one of ours?'

'MI5. I've seen him in Curzon Street.'

'How many others with him?'

'One other, for sure.'

'Recognise him, too?'

'No.'

'I don't suppose you have any idea why they're watching you?' Lockwood asked in a lazy voice.

'If you could tell me why I'm being kept on ice,' replied Hinkley sharply, 'I might have an answer to that.'

'There's still flak over the hijacking business. We're having to conduct an investigation into *your* incompetence. You're the scapegoat, old boy. That's my reading of it. You mustn't worry unduly. *I* am your boss. I *am* the Iberian Desk. Nothing will happen without them first consulting me, and I shall clear you.'

'So what do *I* do, boss?' Hinkley asked peevishly.

Lockwood was now screwing a long lens onto the camera he had brought from downstairs.

'Wait and see, old boy,' was his wry reply. 'It's what we do best.'

Lockwood photographed the watcher-in-the-shadows across the street.

'Now,' he said, breaking the mood. 'I'll have this chap's particulars first thing in the morning.'

On the train back to Chelsea, Hinkley was able to confirm that his 'escort' numbered two men. They made no attempt to conceal their purpose.

They followed him to his door, keeping forty paces behind. Their relief team – a man and a woman – kept watch on the house from their car throughout the night.

At about 3 AM, Hinkley entered Mary's bedroom and woke her. He made her put on her dressing gown and slippers. He wouldn't speak to her, except to insist that she follow him downstairs.

She followed.

He led her out into the back yard.

'The men who fixed the central heating, did they work only in the out-house?' he asked her.

'Who?' Mary replied. She was still not fully conscious.

'The central-heating men. Did they check all the radiators? What rooms were they in?'

'I don't know,' said Mary. 'I don't remember. It's awfully cold out here. What time is it?'

'Think!' he demanded. 'Which rooms were they in?'

He embraced her to warm her. The embrace felt strange to her – excessively tight – but she responded similarly.

'Did you watch them?' he asked.

'I don't remember which rooms they were in, Jack. Is that why you brought me out here: to ask me that? What *is* the matter?'

'Never mind,' said Hinkley. 'Go back to bed.'

He had not yet released her.

'What time is it? Do you want me to make tea?'

'It's late. Just go to bed.'

Finally, he let go of her. Reluctantly, she returned to her room. Already, she had forgotten why Jack had woken her.

Hinkley searched until dawn. In all, he found four bugs. One in the living room. One in the kitchen. One in the dining room. One in the spare bedroom. He assumed that the telephone was tapped, and that there was a device in Mary's room. (He didn't want to waken her again, so he had left the search of the master bedroom until later.) He would assume he had missed others. He recognised it as the work of the surveillance department in Camberwell. Hinkley speculated that they would have cut off the central heating at the tank in the out-house, monitored the telephone calls so as to intercept the call Mary would make to the heating contractors. They would have then cancelled the appointment Mary had made with the contractors, and turned up themselves in boiler-suits drawn from the wardrobe at Camberwell.

Once again, he sat in the living room with only the light from the street-lamp for illumination. He switched on the record-player. The Berlin Philharmonic Orchestra would shield his thoughts. He concentrated on recalling his contribution to conversations in the house since returning. He could think of nothing that could be construed as damaging, but he was sickened to think of them listening in Mary's bedroom.

Five hundred miles away, in Zurich, someone else had had a sleepless night. Mikka's wife had been to the police. A missing-person's file had been opened on Mikka in the Swiss city where he lived with his family, and where his one-man law practice had its registered office. It would be an extensive investigation. Mikka also had a flat in Prague and a postal address in West Berlin. There was nothing unusual about him being away from his wife and children for a week or more at a time, but he was a doting husband and father. He never failed to telephone once a day while he was abroad; never, that is, until now. His wife had made her own exhaustive enquiries. No one had seen him for four days or more.

★

The sewage-flow in the apartment block in Moscow had improved. The drains outside were clear again. The vile smell lingered, though it had dissipated. The city-appointed engineer had called off an inspection of the principal sewage conduit to which the apartment block was connected. He attributed the temporary blockage to misuse of the plumbing facilities in the building, and solemnly advised the occupants to refrain from treating the system as a means of garbage-disposal.

'It's simple,' he boomed at the building supervisor, 'they put their rubbish in the bins and the plumbing will last forever.' He gave a big, hollow laugh.

4

'You were right,' said Hinkley. 'Snitkina is in Amsterdam.'

'We keep close tabs on that guy,' replied Baxter.

They kept a moderate pace down Regent Street.

'Why aren't you in Amsterdam?' asked Hinkley. 'You're not on the embassy payroll here, are you?' He knew damn well he was.

'The President has a job for me in London,' said Baxter solemnly. 'He's got me watching hippies, guys worried about getting cancer from coloured toilet paper.'

'All right. So I shouldn't have asked.'

'Why haven't they sent you back to Barcelona?' countered Baxter. 'They still mad at you?'

'Something like that.'

'Still can't help me on Paris?'

'Sorry, Otis.'

'Nothing at all on Klinovec?'

'I never said we saw Klinovec in Barcelona. *You* said *your* lot saw him.'

'Hell, I never said you saw him. I just thought you guys might have picked up a scrap in Paris we missed.'

Baxter sighed, as though it didn't really matter.

'So where have you been that has you so uptight?' he asked Hinkley.

'I've been to my tailor.'

'Your tailor!' exclaimed Baxter. He liked the idea, but he couldn't imagine Jack having a tailor.

'To be measured for a suit.'

'What's with the suit? Haven't you got enough suits?'

'I felt good in the morning-suit I wore to Vanessa's wedding. I've just had my monthly cheque paid into my account, so I decided to purchase a new suit. Is that all right with you?'

'I thought you English never paid your tailors.'

'Some have gentlemen's credit,' said Hinkley severely.

'They're the guys who don't pay?'

'They wait and see, Otis.'

'What's with the minders?' Baxter asked casually.

The question served as a reminder to Hinkley that his American friend was not the buffoon he pretended to be.

'They haven't decided whether I'm an asset or a liability,' was the bitter reply.

'They must be *real* mad,' said Baxter. 'Still, they haven't stopped your cheque.'

'Where's that drink you promised?'

Hinkley returned to the house in Chelsea drunk. He wasn't rowdy. He was alcohol-soaked. Maudlin. At first, he wouldn't speak to Mary. Mary was already distraught, having come from visiting her brother.

'What's the matter with you, Jack?' She put her hand on his arm, but he pulled away.

'How is Geoffrey?' he enquired miserably.

'He's not at all well. Will you come to the hospital with me again this evening?'

'Do you want me to?'

'Of course I do.'

'Then I will.'

'Do you want some coffee?'

'I'll make it myself.'

Hinkley sat alone in the kitchen and reviewed the conversation he had had with his friend Baxter in the pub. Baxter wasn't interested in Snitkina. Of that, he was sure. His sniffing around for scraps concerned Hinkley. The CIA would have got whatever they needed on Snitkina from Pickering through their liaison officer if Century House had something they didn't. Baxter was interrogating him. Where did Baxter's conversation with Lockwood fit in? Hinkley trusted Lockwood, but his studied evasiveness the night before bothered him. *Wait and see, old boy.* It was they who were waiting. Waiting for Hinkley's move. Clearly, it was more than an investigation into one officer's alleged incompetence. The surveillance team and the bugging devices attested to that. What treachery had he committed? Perhaps when his head cleared he would be able to determine the connection between his learning of the identity of C's mole in Moscow, the unfortunate blunder in Barcelona, and the untenable position in which he now found himself.

Instead of making coffee, he poured himself another drink.

★

Mary had arranged to meet Vanessa and Roger at the hospital. The couple wanted to visit Uncle Geoffrey before departing on their honeymoon.

The nurse asked that all four not visit together. The newly-weds went in first. They had a plane to catch. They weren't allowed to stay long. Vanessa cried in the corridor when she came out of the ward. Her mother comforted her.

Hinkley did what he thought was expected of him. 'How are you getting to the airport?' he asked his son-in-law.

'I don't want to leave the car at Heathrow. We've got a taxi waiting outside with our things in it.'

'Your old man gave you a lift up to London?'

'We took the taxi.'

'From Canterbury?'

'Well yes.'

'Why didn't you stay with us last night? We would have left you alone.'

In truth, Hinkley had good reason to be glad they hadn't stayed in Chelsea. 'Christ, a taxi from Canterbury. I'll drive you the rest of the way.'

'You will not,' interjected Mary. 'He's not driving you, Roger. He's not in a fit state to drive.'

'I'm bloody all right,' her offended husband replied loudly.

'Dad, please,' said Vanessa. She embraced him. 'We could still postpone the honeymoon.'

'What for?' her father demanded, in the same loud voice.

'For Geoffrey,' retorted Mary. Suddenly, Mary let go. 'You come back here expecting everything to be the same as when you left. You certainly behave as if nothing has changed. I can't have a conversation with you. You've nothing to say. You're so wrapped up in your damn secret world, you haven't noticed my brother is dying.'

'Don't say that,' pleaded Vanessa. 'We don't know.'

Hinkley was surprised by his wife's public outburst, and shocked by the word 'dying', but what Mary had to say of his attentions was, of course, true, and he knew it.

Mary fought to hold back tears.

'You go, my sweet,' she said to Vanessa. 'Take her now, Roger. You don't want to be late for your flight.'

Once she had composed herself, Mary led the way into the ward.

Geoffrey was very low. He was drawn. They had made it so. Better that than the pain. The operation, and attendant complications, had aged him terribly. He didn't recognise Mary and Jack at first. Mary sat on the edge of the bed and stroked his hand.

'Come on, Geoffrey,' said Hinkley foolishly, 'you're not going to let this end it all.'

'Get out of here, Jack,' Mary said in a low, anguished voice.

Geoffrey still hadn't identified his visitors. He was muttering something about a honeymoon when Hinkley walked out.

143

★

Hinkley caused a disturbance outside the intensive-care unit. He insisted that he see the surgeon who had performed the operation on his brother-in-law. When he got no satisfaction, he became violent. He struck a hospital porter to the floor. The police were called, but the matter was resolved by the time they had arrived. Hinkley had apologised. Mary, too, had apologised on her husband's behalf. She explained that he was under considerable stress as a result of his brother-in-law's condition. The explanation was accepted in good faith.

Afterwards, Mary was utterly ashamed of having used her brother's illness as an excuse for her husband's inexcusable aggression.

Once again, Jack Hinkley felt sick. He could see it for what it was – another appalling act – only this time there was no benefit to be had. It was another shameful moment in a long line of shameful moments throughout an undistinguished life.

Part Four

1

The telephone rang at 7.45 AM. It was the call Hinkley had been waiting for. He was summoned to Pickering's West End flat.

'A car has been sent,' said the caller.

The car was already in the street. It had been there all night. The surveillance team had merely double-parked outside Hinkley's door.

'Morning,' said Hinkley, once he had pulled the door closed.

'Morning,' both men replied in turn.

'Mind if I smoke?' asked Hinkley, already reaching into his pocket.

'No, go ahead,' said the other passenger.

Hinkley lit up.

'Heavy traffic,' said one, when they were obliged to stop repeatedly on Buckingham Palace Road.

'Bloody awful,' replied the other. He was gripey. He wanted his breakfast.

The previous surveillance pair was altogether more human, more impatient. These were old dogs. Their guts were slow. Breakfast could wait.

Hinkley gave a rackety cough. It was his first cigarette of the day. His cough seemed worse in a stationary car than at the breakfast table. His companions watched unsympathetically. Hinkley wanted to establish that the lack of sympathy was mutual.

'Don't you fellows shave?' he asked when he had recovered.

Neither answered.

Nothing more was said until they reached the entrance to the building on Jermyn Street.

Both men got out of the car with their charge.

'I know where to go,' said Hinkley.

They insisted on escorting him upstairs to the flat. They made their delivery, then left to guard the entrance.

Pickering and Lockwood were waiting for Hinkley inside. Pickering, a bachelor, lived in modest quarters on the second floor. Two rooms knocked together, a small bedroom, a kitchen no bigger than the pokey bathroom. The place was cluttered with heavy furniture and hardback books without dustjackets.

It was Pickering who answered the door. Lockwood was standing by one of the two windows that overlooked Jermyn Street. He had a cup and saucer in his hand, and he was uncomfortable. It was the uneasiness he had exhibited in his own house in Richmond when Hinkley had called – only now, Hinkley had a theory that seemed to fit the circumstances. He'd been up all night thinking about it.

He had seen it done before: isolating a suspected double-agent. The kid-glove treatment from colleagues under orders to maintain contact with the suspect while denying him access to documents, retreating, if challenged. He had seen the guilty first seize up, then crack under the strain of not knowing how much the firm knew. It was a further application of the wait-and-see business Lockwood championed.

Soviet and Eastern Bloc defectors were treated similarly. Zeisler had fallen victim to it in Munich. They had deliberately treated him as a defector. They had welcomed him warmly, but they had also hinted at a comprehensive knowledge of his delinquent behaviour. They had dressed him in expensive clothes, then made oblique references to a catalogue of compromising photographs.

So, this meeting in Pickering's flat was to be the first interrogation. Hinkley was eager to begin. Whether suspected double-agent or defector, the firm forever withheld its blessing once it harboured doubts. It was a stark reality Hinkley was prepared to face, for there was more than his future career at stake. If he had judged his predicament correctly – ludicrous though it was – there was now a charge of treason to be answered.

There was a third man present. Bradshaw, Pickering's opposite number at MI5. He, too, had a cup of tea. His was rested on the arm of the couch on which he sat.

Hinkley had expected C to be present because, so far as he knew, C was the only person who was in possession of the full facts of the case. On a superficial level, given that the firm suspected Hinkley of being a double-agent, there was good reason for MI5's involvement in their primary capacity as spy-catchers, but under the circumstances the matter should not have gone beyond the walls of C's office.

MI5 hadn't instigated the enquiry. According to Lockwood, it was Pickering who was briefing Bradshaw, not the other way round.

'Tea?' Pickering asked abruptly.

'No thank you,' replied Hinkley.

'Lost your taste for it in Barcelona, I dare say.' Pickering managed to make it sound like a betrayal. 'Sit down.' He pointed to a hard chair which was turned outwards form the dining table.

Hinkley sat. Lockwood's uneasiness seemed more pronounced when viewed from a seated position.

'Jack,' began Pickering, 'sometimes our boys and girls are overworked. They're always under strain. If they haven't leart to relax, they're apt to do something out of character.' He stopped to punctuate his remarks by raising his eyebrows. 'Now I don't see this being the cause of the incident at the Royal Marsden Hospital yesterday,' he said dismissively. 'Perhaps you'd be good enough to tell us what happened?'

As beginnings went, Pickering's was hardly indulgent.

Pickering was accusing Hinkley of unprofessional conduct, and Hinkley had no acceptable excuse to offer. He could think of no evasive ploy, so he was frank.

'It was personal. It shouldn't have happened. I'd been drinking.'

'We know that,' interjected Pickering sharply.

'*I* haven't been able to relax.'

'Ah yes . . . ' Pickering again interrupted, 'the Barcelona affair.'

'I don't like being watched.' Hinkley made a point of engaging Bradshaw's gaze.

'How is your brother-in-law?' continued Pickering.

'Dying, perhaps.'

'I'm sorry to hear it.'

Pickering paced the Persian carpet for a moment, then stopped abruptly. It was another of those little actions he felt he had to perform. This one seemed to say: I'm on home ground; you're not.

'The Barcelona affair is closed. There was an understandable miscalculation on your part. Larch's death is a separate matter.' Pickering spoke fast. His three short statements knocked Hinkley off balance, sent him spinning.

'So why am I being followed?'

'We're not interested in you, Jack,' said Bradshaw. The voice was gruffer than Hinkley had expected of a man who so carefully posied his cup and saucer on what was a narrow couch-arm. 'It's your friend, Otis Baxter, we're watching,' he concluded.

'So why have you got my house bugged?'

Understandably, there was a brief silence.

'Look, Jack,' said Lockwood, 'they had to be sure . . . .'

'Sure? Sure of what?'

'That you weren't working with him,' replied Lockwood candidly. 'Otis Baxter is working for Moscow Centre. He has been for at least three years. They recruited him in Washington. We know a lot about him now. He's a clumsy chap.'

Hinkley was unprepared for this new twist.

'Don't worry,' said Pickering churlishly, 'you haven't let us down. You didn't let anything slip. We'd know if you had.'

'He's seen your scruffs,' Hinkley said in a bitter aside to Bradshaw.

'He thinks we're watching you,' replied Bradshaw smugly. 'And we were,' he added.

'I want you to run through the conversation you had with him in the Criterion Bar yesterday,' said Pickering.

'Don't you have it on tape?'

Pickering didn't like his insolence, but then Hinkley didn't much care for the way he had been used.

'I can understand your annoyance,' he said patronisingly, 'but I expect your cooperation.'

If Hinkley could believe them, there was cause for some relief. It was a briefing rather than an interrogation. Otis Baxter a Soviet agent? It might explain why Moscow never swallowed the Zeisler story. If, somehow, Baxter had known all along about the photographic session in the Hamburg brothel, it would explain a lot. When Zeisler disappeared, Moscow would have had good reason to suspect he had been abducted. Baxter would have already told his Soviet controller that Zeisler had been targeted for blackmail. If Baxter was uncovered just after that, it would explain why the photographs were never used. Such a scenario would confirm that the Zeisler operation – from start to finish – was a waste.

'Well?' said Pickering impatiently.

'He asked about Barcelona. He said he'd never been there. He wanted to know if the women in Barcelona were like the mulatto women in Cuba.'

'What was your reply?' asked Pickering earnestly.

'I said I'd never been to Cuba.'

152

'Go on.'

'He said Cuban women expected a man to wear clean clothes, polished shoes and aftershave. Even the fat ones with curlers under their headscarves. They'd tell you if they thought you needed a shower. He said they liked to see a man's hair wet.'

'And you said?'

'And I said, "Why don't you visit me in Barcelona?"'

'He replied . . . ?'

'That he would.'

'Go on.'

'We ordered drinks. He asked the barman to make him a mojito. You know . . . rum, lemon juice, sugar and soda with mint leaves and ice . . . ' He was glad to see Pickering was getting just a little more impatient, while still keeping it in check.

'You both had mojitos?'

'No.'

'What did you drink?'

'A Scotch.'

'Double?'

'Which brand?'

'Glenfiddich.'

'A single Scotch.'

'Go on.'

'He asked about my daughter's wedding.'

'Elaborate.'

'He asked how it went.'

'How it went?'

'How many attended? What business my son-in-law's family was in? What the food was like? He was very interested in the food. When he heard there was fish on the menu, he asked if it was served with marsh samphire. He said smart London restaurants had begun to use marsh samphire as a fish garnish. He asked whether or not I liked my son-in-law. What business was he in. How much did I pay for the hire of my morning-suit.'

'You answered all his questions?'

'Yes.'

'What were your answers?'

'I said there were about a hundred and twenty at the service, sixty at the reception, that the family made its money on the stock exchange, that a lot of money had been spent on a firm of caterers, that the fish wasn't garnished with marsh samphire. I told him my son-in-law didn't need to work and probably didn't intend working.'

'Did you tell Baxter you liked the boy?'

'I said I might change my mind.'

'By that, I assume you meant you might grow to like him?'

'Yes.'

'Baxter made the same assumption?'

'He didn't ask me to elaborate,' said Hinkley darkly.

'That's all about the wedding?'

'Yes.'

'Continue.'

'He had asked me earlier about the suit I'm having made. He asked again. He asked how soon it would be ready.'

'You replied . . . ?'

'Ten days. My tailor had said he was busy.'

'Is that all about the suit?'

'He asked if it was flannel, on account of the heat in Barcelona. I said it was mohair. I'd be wearing it in the evenings.'

'Anything more about the suit?'

'No. That brought us back to Barcelona. He pressed me for information on Snitkina.'

'Were you still on your first drink?'

'Yes.'

'Go on.'

'He asked me if I wanted to go fishing before I left for Barcelona. He said he had a spare rod. He said my minders would look pretty damn stupid hiding behind a tree. I said I hadn't the time nor the inclination.'

'Then?'

'Then he asked about Barcelona again, about the follow-up to the hijacking. He had already told me that Langley believed Major Klinovec was on the flight, but that they didn't know who he was meeting in Paris. He again implied that we also knew he was on the flight. Again he asked had we picked up anything in Paris. He said they had reason to believe there was some connection – possibly financial – between Klinovec and the recent bomb campaign.'

'A red herring,' said Pickering dismissively.

'That's what I thought. He was pressing hard for information. He was in a hurry.'

'So he got quickly to the point?'

'Yes.'

'You were suspicious from the outset?'

'Yes.'

'You didn't tell Lockwood of your suspicions. You didn't approach me. Why?'

155

'I assumed he was doing some detective work for you. I had found Mr Bradshaw's devices.' The sardonic tone in Hinkley's voice was unmistakable.

'How many drinks had you had by then?'

'Two.'

'What was his second?'

'Mojito.'

'And yours?'

'Scotch. Single. Glenfiddich.'

'He wanted to know more about events immediately following the hijacking. Continue.'

'I repeated what I had told him: there was no fourth man.'

'Did he ask about Larch?'

'Not on that occasion. He did mention Larch once. He said that the CIA had Snitkina's apartment bugged, that Snitkina had had a visitor the night of the hijacking, that they believed the visitor was Klinovec, and suggested that Larch had followed Klinovec to the apartment where he was killed.'

'Two mysteries our cousins have answers for. What do you make of that?'

'Klinovec wasn't in the place. Larch was mugged. It's in the report.'

'Yes. I've read the report. Go on.'

'He again offered to take me fishing. I repeated that I hadn't time.'

'That was it?'

'He wanted to go night-clubbing.'

'When?'

'That evening.'

'You turned him down?'

'Yes.'

'But you had another drink?'

'Yes.'

'Then you went to the Royal Marsden Hospital drunk?'

The hectoring Pickering was determined to establish Hinkley's complete lack of self-control. Pickering knew damn well that Hinkey hadn't gone straight to the hospital.

'No, I went home first. Then I went to the hospital drunk.'

Hinkley knew Pickering wanted to be able to say: 'I told you, gentleman, he doesn't belong with us.'

Lockwood, who had remained silent and standing, as if somehow to counter the spitefulness of Pickering, spoke up.

'Snitkina is sitting in Amsterdam waiting to hear from Baxter, Jack. What exactly he's expecting, we've not yet established, but it must be of importance for Snitkina to be personally involved, and for Baxter to take these kinds of risks, approaching you as he has.'

'Baxter may be clumsy,' continued Bradshaw, 'but he isn't stupid. He knows we're on to him. He's brazen enough to attempt to finish his business before he's spirited away.'

'You see, we haven't told the CIA of Baxter's treachery,' said Pickering. 'Naturally, we've wanted to keep him in play for as long as possible. Now, we must make our move. I want you to meet him again.'

'Why not just pick him up?' asked Hinkley.

'He's already gone to ground,' replied Bradshaw.

'Besides,' said Pickering, 'this way we have immediate proof. Something we can show the Americans.'

'Catch him red-handed, as it were,' said Hinkley mockingly.

'Exactly,' replied Pickering, playing the game. 'Do you know Comfort's Corner?'

'Yes, I know it.'

Comfort's Corner was a site in the older part of Highgate Cemetery that had in the past been used as a meeting-place by the firm. It was so named not after an abstract, but merely as the site of a cluster of tombs bearing the family name: Comfort.

'Meet him there,' said Pickering.

'You're assuming he'll contact me,' said Hinkley.

'They're desperate for information. Baxter's controller is pushing him hard. He'll try again. We must find out what they're after.'

'If he's gone to ground, he might risk a phone call,' said Hinkley. 'He won't agree to meet. You've said it yourself: he knows we're on to him.'

'Tell him you talked to Miss Garetti. Tell him you have something you picked up in Paris.'

'Who's Garetti?'

'A talent-spotter. Moscow sometimes uses her as a cut-out.'

'You want Baxter to think I've been turned?'

'You're dissatisfied with the treatment you've been getting, aren't you?'

'He won't swallow it. He'll be expecting something like this. He'll check.'

'He knows the net is closing fast. The next time he makes contact with his controller, it will be to arrange his escape.'

'I still say he'll check.'

'If necessary, we can arrange for his controller to be unavailable. He can't possibly know we're on the Garetti as well.'

'He doesn't need to know. He won't take the risk.'

Pickering allowed a beat before issuing his order: 'If Baxter calls, you'll arrange to meet him.'

'*If* he calls,' replied Hinkley sharply. 'Is this the sole reason I've been kept in London: my association with Baxter?'

'There is no longer any confusion surrounding the follow-up operation to the hijacking, if that's what you're referring to,' said Pickering. 'Larch's death still has to be thoroughly investigated.'

'When do I go back to Barcelona to conduct the investigation?'

'When you've finished here,' retorted Pickering.

'He didn't like Hinkley's insolence. It was a crude, combative ploy.

'Is that really why you bugged my house, Mr Bradshaw?' asked Hinkley over his shoulder. 'In case Otis Baxter called?'

'We told you why,' replied Bradshaw evasively.

'You put a bug in my bedroom in case Otis Baxter called?' asked Hinkley. He was furious.

'He's sleeping with your wife,' Pickering said matter-of-factly.

Hinkley was dumbfounded.

In the moment between closing the door and starting down the staircase, Hinkley's silence begged an answer to the question: did you know? The answer was in Lockwood's downcast eyes.

'I'm sorry, Jack.'

They descended the staircase without further exchange. In the doorway, Lockwood paused to put on his leather gloves. Again, he spoke. 'Nothing is private, Jack. It may be secret, but it's not private.'

The comment wasn't designed to comfort. It was simply Lockwood's way of saying there was no room for embarrassment or shame.

2

There was nothing to be said. Not yet, at any rate. In Hinkley's limited experience personal loss was best not spoken about or allowed to fester, and that meant there was no reason for regret. Hurt was to be evenly spun out over time, and always without confiding in others.

He sat waiting for another call; waiting for deliverance.

The Otis Baxter briefing had come as a shock and on the back of it Pickering had cast Hinkley as an artless plodder – which, under the circumstances, seemed perfectly reasonable – and yet . . . Hinkley was not convinced that the sole purpose for his being kept in London under surveillance was to bait Baxter.

Hinkley would play Pickering's game. He would lure Baxter into a trap if Baxter was foolish enough to make contact, but he would remain alert to undeclared interest.

Hinkley had done as C had ordered: he had kept his mouth shut about Klinovec. He was now thinking that just perhaps, the abortive operation he had led in Barcelona had stopped short of disaster. The emergency debate in the House of Commons had been delayed to accommodate recommendations made by the TREVI committee and the EEC meeting of Interior Ministers. Nothing that would be said at the emergency debate could prove more damaging, unintentionally or otherwise, than that which had already been voiced at the TREVI and EEC meetings. Running for cover under the cannot-be-disclosed umbrella, as Lockwood had put it, might cause several Members considerable discomfort, but it was better than admitting that they weren't in possession of the full facts.

It took all of Hinkley's strength to sit still. Even if it was as simple as Pickering had made out, he would have to wait until Baxter had been caught, or it had been established that he had made good his escape. Hinkley had Bradshaw's scruffs for company. They continued to watch and to eavesdrop. The boiler-men from Camberwell came to remove devices when Mary was out teaching. They had made an appointment with Hinkley to do so. Hinkley watched them at work. That didn't bother them. They were finished in ten minutes.

Though he could find no new bugs when they had left, Hinkley knew the bastards still got to hear what he said in his sleep.

In Moscow, Klinovec, the man who so desperately needed Hinkley's silence, didn't dare think he was in the clear. Not yet. Vigodskaya had been going through the files at Moscow Centre, systematically scrutinising each case Klinovec had been involved in since his induction. Klinovec was confident that he would turn up nothing incriminating. However, Klinovec now knew that it had been a mistake to go to Snitkina in Barcelona. He had learnt that Vigodskaya was waiting for a report from Snitkina in Amsterdam. He knew that intensive enquiries were being conducted in London by Soviet agents. He knew that if he were to be betrayed, it would be there.

As for the slaying of Mikka, the Second Directorate had been following closely the missing-person reports in several Western newspapers. There hadn't been more than a paragraph or two, and a photograph, in each article. The papers may not have carried anything about the missing lawyer, had it not been for the efforts of the Swiss police to have the man's photograph published. A few bright journalists, smelling yet another sordid spy story, were eager to follow it up, but thus far had been unable to establish the circumstances of his disappearance. The police, it seemed, had no real clues.

Moscow's silent interest had been prompted by the discovery of the car Mikka had hired in Moscow. It had been sitting idle near the Stadium for Young Pioneers for several days now. Moscow Centre was waiting for someone to collect it.

Back in London, Hinkley was climbing the walls in the house in Chelsea. He switched on the answering-maching and left.

He telephoned Barbara deWitt on her direct line at Century House. He intended asking her out to lunch. He wanted to compare her briefing on Baxter with his own. Like Lockwood, Barbara deWitt was a colleague of long standing. She was another gatherer: in Hinkley's estimation, a gatherer with skills far superior to his own. She understood the communal mind better than anyone, except perhaps C, but unlike C, she was not a fanatical schemer. Hinkley was confident he would be capable of detecting any extraordinary reserve on her part – a reserve that would suggest there was an ulterior motive at work. Alas, he could ask for nothing more. As it was, it would be as crude as Baxter's approach to him had been. The irony did not escape Hinkley.

It wasn't Barbara who answered the telephone. Barbara wasn't in the office at the moment. Could a message be left, or the call returned?

No.

Hinkley rang Barbara's home number. There was no reply. He was ringing from a public telephone in Victoria Station. He went down into the Underground and caught the next District train bound for Richmond. He alighted at Kew Gardens. His escort trailed conspicuously twenty yards behind on the suburban avenue that linked the station with the Public Records Office. Lockwood had said that Barbara had been working in Kew. She was probably reviewing material soon to be made public under the thirty-year rule. There had been complaints from politicians, journalists and academics about the editing of sensitive material released under the disclosure rule. Within the Foreign Office itself, there had been complaints as to the crudity of that editing, It was time to get rid of the circus elephant's typewriter: that was the joke. It was not surprising that, unofficially, Barbara deWitt had now been given the task.

In the main reading room on the first floor, Hinkley asked for her by name at the enquiry desk. She had to come from another part of the building. He left his own name, and said he would wait in the canteen downstairs.

There was a lunchtime queue. Hinkley bought a coffee from a vending-machine.

Barbara was prompt.

'Lunch?' she asked.

'No. But you must have something.'

'I have three plump Moroccan oranges in my bag upstairs. You'll have one of those?'

'No thanks, Barbara.'

She looked to his plastic cup.

'I'll just have tea,' she said, as if to facilitate his schedule. She, too, bought from the vending machine. She pressed the button for extra sugar. She didn't bother with a spoon.

'I rang you at your desk,' said Hinkley as she sat down. 'Then I tried your home number. When there was no reply there, I thought you might be out here.'

'There's nobody at home,' said Barbara. 'Denis is away on business, and I've sent Alice and Elizabeth to the richer of their two grandmothers.'

Hinkley's face broke into a nervous smile.

'How is Mary?' continued Barbara.

'Mary is fine.' The smile had vanished.

'And Vanessa?'

'Married. Also fine.'

Barbara sighed in polite approval.

'I didn't know. I'm a little out of touch here.'

She waited. She wasn't going to ask why Hinkley had come.

Hinkley was ill at ease. Through the glass partition, he could see one of his escorts seated in the foyer. Barbara picked up on it immediately.

'Is it just because we're part of it, or are they really that conspicuous?'

'You know why they're following me?'

Already, Hinkley had thrown caution to the wind.

'Frankly, no.'

'Otis Baxter is working for Moscow,' he blurted out. 'You must know that. They wouldn't have let him near you without briefing you.'

'What if he is?'

'What did they tell you about him?'

DeWitt's knowledge of Baxter was the same as his, if he could believe her.

'What about me, Barbara?' Now Hinkley was being indiscreet. He was exhibiting all the signs of a man whose nerve was progressively giving way. 'Why am I out in the cold?'

'Well, I haven't been told not to talk to you, if that's a help.'

It was hopeless. It had been foolish of Hinkley to imagine that he would be any closer to the whole truth by talking to deWitt. She was probably responsible for much of the misinformation that had been fed to Baxter since he had been uncovered.

'I'm sorry, Barbara, I shouldn't be asking questions.'

'No, you shouldn't,' she said, trying to be kind. 'You won't be satisfied with the answers. Now, bugger MI5. Have an orange.'

Another cheerless smile.

'All right.'

When Barbara returned with her oranges, she found that Hinkley had left.

3

Hinkley was watching the main evening news bulletin on television. The 'security alert' was still a major item. There were images of a city expecting bombs. *Police wish to interview this man in connection with the Paris bombing.* There was a photograph taken from a passport.

The cricket results were on the screen when the telephone rang. It was Baxter. He wanted Hinkley to come out to play.

'Can you believe it, Jack? I got a bunch of reporters banging on my door asking if it's true. . . . "If what's true?" I ask. "If he's gotten married." "If who's gotten married?" The goddamn rock star next door. They got a TV crew out there, now. You can't get rid of these guys. They're sitting on my doorstep. What do you say we go for a drink?'

'I don't think so.'

'What about that place we've been to once before – remember – smokey and dark. You need radar to cross the floor . . . .'

'I'm sorry, Otis. Not tonight. What about tomorrow? Are you free tomorrow?'

'Can't tomorrow.'

'What about your pal, Garetti? Ring her. She's single.'

There was only the slightest hesitation at the other end of the line.

'Why not the three of us?' suggested Baxter.

Hinkley could hear Baxter's brain churning: *he* hadn't introduced Hinkley to Garetti. Garetti had never met him in anyone's company. Garetti was an emergency cut-out.

'Tomorrow, Otis. I'm spending an evening with Mary.'

Baxter agreed to meet the following day.

'If you're going to choke your lungs in some dive tonight,' said Hinkley, 'let's get some fresh air in the morning.'

They agreed to meet on Parliament Hill on Hampstead Heath. From there, it was a comfortable walk to Highgate Cemetery. Hinkley wanted a little extra time with his friend, Otis Baxter.

'Who was it?' asked Mary.

'It wasn't for you,' Hinkley replied.

4

The grass grew. Swimmers swam in the Lido. A bitter wind cut across Parliament Hill and swept down to chill the city. The chill awakened misgivings in Hinkley that he had surpressed since the disastrous Zeisler affair. The blindness which he now suffered was a corporate thing. The firm wanted him that way. Barbara deWitt was right: he would not be satisfied with answers his colleagues gave. Not now. Not until this particular game had been played out. Others had talent. He had courage. Besides, who in the firm was in possession of a comprehensive picture of activities? The whole thing ran on trust: trust that in the end, one was safe.

Hinkley arrived late, Baxter later still – or so it appeared. He had probably been watching from a distance, from cover. It was too gusty for kites, but there was a kite-flyer, a boy of twelve, his bicycle thrown on its side, its pedal embedded in the grass. There was Hinkley. No one else within six hundred yards.

Baxter approached from the South End Green direction. It wasn't his usual gait. He was plodding. Perhaps it was the slope, or the gusting wind, or his preoccupation with the fruit he was eating.

Hinkley was standing. He was slightly taller than Baxter. Sitting, Baxter filled more seat. Unlike Hinkley, he was a natural sitter. Hinkley stood, because he wanted the advantage.

'Hi there,' said Baxter, with a broad American smile.

For the moment, Hinkley remained silent. He surveyed the low urban horizon. Baxter took up a position at his side. He offered a grape.

'No thanks,' said Hinkley.

Baxter ate the grape himself.

'Get rid of your reporters, did you?' asked Hinkley.

'No. They're still camped outside. They won't believe he's in the States. I told them I might be able to organise a photograph of his dog. They didn't like that. Now I think they're staying to spite me. The guy next door gets married and I get to suffer.'

Baxter shuffled his feet. The cold had penetrated his raincoat, to reach his layer of fat.

'How do you like this weather?' Baxter complained. 'They say it's going to get colder, too.'

Hinkley made no reply.

'OK,' said Baxter, 'I've seen enough. Can I buy you a coffee?'

'You should have told me,' Hinkley said, his eyes still set on the horizon. He was choking with indignation.

Baxter quickly inserted several grapes into his mouth.

'About what?'

'About you and Mary.'

Hinkley turned to look at him.

'I can keep a secret,' Baxter replied, chewing hard on the residual skins of his grapes with his front teeth. Otis Baxter treated his stomach as though it was an invalid pet. He fed it constantly. He stroked it. Now that Hinkley had found out about his affair with Mary, he would have to chew everything twice to avoid upsetting his stomach.

Hinkley wasn't shocked by the callousness of the reply. The reply could easily be interpreted as: *You walked out on her. What do you expect?*

'Mary and I are very fond of each other,' said Baxter. 'You understand.'

Baxter wasn't intimidated by the eye-contact.

Yes, Hinkley understood. Baxter wasn't big enough to lie, and say that he loved her.

'You took advantage of her, and you took advantage of our friendship.'

Hinkley knew that his was not a legitimate grievance. How could it be? He had taken advantage of Baxter in Hamburg. The difference was that Baxter didn't know it.

'Like I've said, I really like her. I wouldn't have met her if we hadn't known each other, so I guess you're right. I've been taking advantage of you both.'

'You should have told me.'

'Come on, Jack. The hell I should have told you. I didn't want to hurt your feelings. You want me to stop seeing her?'

Hinkley made no reply, but started to walk.

'There's a coffee shop back there,' said Baxter. 'They've got Italian pastries.'

Hinkley was already on his set course for Highgate Cemetery.

Baxter followed him.

There was another offer of grapes.

Another refusal.

'Is that what you wanted to talk about? Mary?' asked Baxter, like some disappointed businessman.

Hinkley wanted to jolt this cocky bastard.

'Do you know that MI5 has tapes of you screwing my wife?'

It was enough to make Baxter change the rhythm of his jaws.

'They got you bugged?'

'I know why you were sleeping with Mary. They know, too.'

'What's that supposed to mean?' Baxter asked, pushing more grapes into his mouth.

'You were fucking for information, Otis. You see what I mean about taking advantage of Mary?'

Baxter swallowed the contents of his mouth prematurely, and gave an incredulous guffaw. It was convincing. 'Now, just what information is Mary going to give me, Jack?'

'Information about me.'

'Jack, old buddy, there is nothing about you that the US Government needs to know.' Baxter gave an amused, indulgent sigh, and resumed his grape-eating. 'Go on. Let's hear it all.'

'We're going to meet Garetti. Right now. It's been arranged.'

'Have you got something for me on Paris?'

'No. Nothing. Can't you walk faster?'

'You're serious about this . . . *plot* against you, aren't you?'

'Stop acting the idiot, Otis. There isn't time.'

'So what are we seeing this Garetti woman for?'

'You know who she is,' said Hinkley irritably.

'Sure I do. She's an Italian diplomat with bad table manners.'

'Your controller is being watched. Garetti's getting you out. Save some grapes for the journey.' he added, as an afterthought.

Suddenly, Baxter's tone changed. 'Why are you doing this, Jack?'

'Orders, Otis.'

'Oh yeah? From the Kremlin, right?' Baxter's mocking voice was hollow.

Hinkley grinned mirthlessly. He stopped abruptly, and turned to Baxter.

'Coming or not? Personally, I don't give a damn.'

The older, now privately managed part of Highgate Cemetery appeared deserted, but its greenness, and its dampness, could conceal the living, and muffle their footsteps.

A trench had been dug in the orange clay of the footpath using a small mechanical earth-mover. The grounds had long been in need of proper drainage. Plastic pipes would soon bear away the water which was still rich in minerals. Today, however, the earth-mover was idle.

Hinkley followed the route he had been assigned at the operations briefing, jointly presided over by Pickering and Bradshaw early that morning.

Baxter had remained silent and solemn for much of the walk to the cemetery, the only emissions from his mouth being grape-pips. An emergency plan had been put into operation. So he believed. The inevitable journey to an uncertain existence in the East had begun. He didn't relish the thought of life in the Soviet Union. Whatever had prompted his change of loyalties, it had not been the attractions of life in Moscow.

The bleak prospect of a redundant future outweighed the surprise at his friend, Jack Hinkley, MI6 Head of Station in Barcelona, being a double-agent. Certainly, the two men had something in common – but not what Baxter thought. Seemingly, both were trusting that information hitherto denied them by their respective services could now be taken at face value. There, the affinity ended.

Bradshaw's men, together with members of the Special Branch, had been in position for some time. When Hinkley and Baxter stopped at Comfort's Corner, the trap was sprung. Baxter knew instantly that he had been betrayed, but did not resist. For Hinkley, Baxter's passive acceptance of his fate served to make his own arrest more of an unpleasant surprise.

That same day, Baxter's KGB controller, an Aeroflot official, was arrested and immediately deported.

In Amsterdam, Snitkina was duly informed of the three arrests. The news came via an anxious Miss Garetti. There was nothing for Snitkina to do but to return to

Moscow and join Vigodskaya in his efforts to uncover
fresh evidence with which to corner Comrade Klinovec.
For Snitkina, the careerist, his successful prosecution of
the purge to date amounted to little without the biggest
prize.

Part Five

1

Hinkley was taken to Bath, to a Ministry of Defence building, formally the Empire Hotel, a grand Victorian structure overlooking the weir. This in itself was an unusual move. He had not been told whether there was to be a debriefing or an interrogation. In effect, he was being held in custody although no charges had been laid, no explanation given. His warders were Bradshaw's lot. He knew that much. They had settled in for a long wait. They shared his suite of three rooms. The window-sashes needed to be replaced. If it wasn't for the drafts, it would have been a comfortable space. If it wasn't for the company, Hinkley might have found it easier to think. He was never left alone. There was always one in the room and one in the corridor.

There was a telephone without a dial. Calls in only. Lockwood telephoned from London.

'There's absolutely nothing to worry about, Jack. We just want you out of play for the moment. I've told Mary you've been called away unexpectedly. You can ring her shortly. It's a bit of a mystery, I agree. A bloody American in the works can cause havoc. We're having to stage a little drama, it seems. Now I do hope those chaps are entertaining you. They can be so dull, so bloody working class.'

'Am I to be interrogated?' Hinkley asked.

'Heavens, no. You'll be fully briefed. We both will. It's come out of C's office. I'm in the dark. Pickering, too.'

'How long a wait?'

'It seems we can't force the pace. I just don't know, Jack.'

In fact, the answer to Hinkley's question lay in Moscow. Klinovec had been ordered to appear before a committee of inquiry chaired by the Director. C's contingency plan, which Klinovec found so unsatisfactory, had been put into operation in anticipation of just such a move.

★

Vigodskaya and Snitkina were reviewing the circumstantial evidence against Klinovec . . . .

So, their man, Baxter, in London, had failed to secure evidence that Klinovec had indeed been on his way to Paris to rendezvous with a British agent. Baxter had subsequently been picked up, together with the man, Hinkley, known to be MI6 Station Head, Barcelona – the one who, unwittingly, was to provide that evidence. Why had both men been arrested?

The files Vigodskaya had pored over had thrown up a pattern of sorts. The talented Major Klinovec, though he rarely failed, had had his share of abortive operations. He had, on occasion, moved too cautiously, and an operation had foundered as a result. Then there were the cases in which he had moved too swiftly. The case of the traitor, Steibelt, for instance. In Berlin, Klinovec had had the man shot on sight – shot unnecessarily. He had had his share of bad luck, too. There was scarcely anything they could point to as being suggestive of treachery, let alone conclusive evidence of such, but perhaps they would be able to trip him up during cross-examination.

That Klinovec had legitimate business in Paris which the Directorate knew nothing about, was in itself suspicious. Doubtless, he would have a convincing explanation.

That Snitkina could confirm that the British agent, Larch, had followed Klinovec to Snitkina's apartment in Barcelona, and had had to be dealt with, in itself proved nothing.

No. The one outstanding piece of evidence was provided by the testimony of the man Snitkina had sent to follow Klinovec – without Klinovec's knowledge or consent – to ensure his safe-conduct out of Barcelona. He had reported that at the train station, Major Klinovec had been taken away by two men, one of whom was later identified as the British agent, Jack Hinkley. Snitkina's man had failed to intervene at the crucial moment, and had subsequently lost them in the city traffic. A regrettable lapse in security, it was agreed – but how then was Klinovec to explain that, thirty-six hours later, he turned up safely in East Berlin?

What of his bruised neck and stiff leg?

These questions would be put to him.

C's contingency plan was relatively simple. In the event of Klinovec being interrogated, he was to freely admit that he had fallen into the hands of two British agents, for neither C nor Klinovec could be sure that his capture had gone unobserved. He was to maintain that he had escaped after a struggle, and that the British now suspected that their man, Hinkley, had let him go deliberately. This would be supported by reports from London that the man Hinkley had been shadowed by MI5 and finally arrested. Why had Klinovec not brought this to the attention of the Directorate? The answer: he had withheld his report when he learnt of the follow-up operation Moscow Centre had mounted in London. He had never trusted Baxter, the double-agent sent by Vigodskaya to discredit him. It was to be Klinovec's contention that MI5 had exploited Baxter, the mercenary, in snaring Hinkley. In duping Hinkley, they had arrested Baxter also, to fool his other paymasters. It was to be virtually a mirror of the truth. Klinovec would insist that his own silence on the matter was essential if Baxter was not to hear from Vigodskaya or his henchman, Snitkina, of Klinovec's suspicions. This way, Klinovec could demonstrate that Vigodskaya was witch-hunting and that the American, Baxter, was a worthless agent.

Klinovec's life was truly in his own hands. He would need all his skills of deception if he was to weather the interrogation and turn the tide on his accuser.

It was a large, functional room, with tall windows, heavily draped. The table was in proportion to the room. A number of candle-bulbs in the chandelier needed to be replaced. The chandelier didn't belong there. It had come from another, grander interior. It hung too low in this room. Even with several expired bulbs, it cast a hard light on the four men seated side by side facing Klinovec across the table. The Director, Vigodskaya, Snitkina and General Malenkov of Military Intelligence, the only one of the four who was in uniform. Malenkov was the unknown quantity. Klinovec had had no dealings with him directly, although he had, on occasion, made polite conversation with him in the Turkish baths. Unlike many of the other security officers and Kremlin officials who visited the baths, he didn't drink with colleagues, nor did he go to the 'safe' brothels. Klinovec would be playing to Malenkov and to the Director.

'Major Klinovec, this committee of inquiry is here today to establish facts relating to your abortive journey to Paris,' said the Director, 'a journey interrupted by his criticisms. In light of a previous hijacking that forced the jet in which you were travelling to land at Barcelona Airport. You understand that you need keep nothing, however delicate, from this committee?'

'I understand.'

'You will please tell us the purpose of your visit to Paris.'

'We are all aware of Major Snitkina's pioneering work in revitalising our foreign missions,' began Klinovec. 'Paris has already had the benefit of his thoroughness and his enthusiasm. He replaced several of our people before moving on to Madrid, and later, Barcelona. Well, I wasn't satisfied with two of the replacements: Mariya Isayeva and Stepan Andreyev. They had a specific brief to update biographical information on activists among the Arab community in Paris. They had singularly failed in this task. It is not surprising that we know nothing of the perpetrators of the latest Paris bombing. I don't need to remind anyone in this room that one day we may need such information . . . .'

'In spite of Major Snitkina having vetted Mariya Isayeva and Stepan Andreyev, you conducted your own inquiry?' the Director asked.

'Mariya Isayeva and Stepan Andreyev are not answerable to Major Snitkina. They are answerable to me.'

'Why did you go to Paris?' interjected Vigodskaya impatiently.

'In my capacity as master pimp, I paid Isayeva and Andreyev a visit to establish the nature of their difficulty.'

'You take unnecessary risks often?' asked Vigodskaya.

'It was not an unnecessary risk,' replied Klinovec, 'nor was it a great risk.'

'What was the nature of Isayeva and Andreyev's difficulties?' Snitkina demanded.

'A lack of intelligence,' replied Klinovec. 'That is to say, they are both idiots.'

The Director was privately amused by Klinovec's irreverence. A shrewd, merciless man, the Director was also given to indulging favourites. Klinovec was availing of an opportunity to demonstrate his patriotism, and to ingratiate himself with the Director at Vigodskaya's expense. As a matter of course, he had at the outset of his Paris venture arranged this alibi for himself. He had, in fact, interviewed Isayeva and Andreyev and left them smarting. They would remember the meeting with Major Klinovec vividly.

'You don't wait long for results,' countered Snitkina. 'They have been in position only four months.'

'Long enough in this instance,' replied Klinovec curtly.

'Another example of using your own initiative?' asked Vigodskaya witheringly.

'I have submitted to you a recommendation in writing that Mariya Isayeva and Stepan Andreyev be relieved of their duty.'

Ironically, Vigodskaya and Snitkina's impetuous probing had helped to ensure that the unflappable Klinovec was in a strong position from the start of his interrogation by committee.

In London, the House of Commons emergency debate had begun. As is normal practice, the Table Office had prevented questions directly relating to MI5 and MI6 from getting on the Order Paper, but Members of the Opposition were not to be deterred from criticising the Government's reticence in matters of national security. The Government spokesman was quick to point out that the Opposition leader had been, and would continue to be, advised by the Prime Minister on matters pertaining to the current threat to security posed by international terrorism. They had discussed in full, measures proposed by the TREVI committee. They had both welcomed the support of EEC Interior Ministers. Although the Prime Minister would make no reference to it in the House, the Opposition leader had, in fact, been brought into contact with C – a relatively rare occurrence.

The Government endeavoured to steer the House towards a general debate on international cooperation in the fight against terrorism. The Opposition attempted to centre the discussion firmly on British involvement in what it termed the fiasco at Barcelona Airport. They referred to allegations made in the press that the decision to storm the British Airways jet immediately it landed had been taken in London – the implication being that the decision had been taken without due consideration of the circumstances. It was as much a ploy to turn a debate on measures to counter international terrorism into a debate on the curtailment of powers exercised by the security services, and to call again for the creation of a body similar to the Senate and Congressional committees, to which the American security services were answerable.

The press claimed to have a 'reliable source' in the Foreign Office. Lord Peacher had lent the press claims credence by quoting the same anonymous source in the Foreign Office voicing his criticisms. In light of previous well-publicised leaks from the Foreign Office, and Lord Peacher's bitter discourse in the House of Lords, the allegations were taken seriously by public and politicians alike.

The Opposition would not be deflected. The debate developed into a confrontation between the Prime Minister and the Shadow Foreign Secretary. The Prime Minister was pressed on the Barcelona hijacking. The Shadow Foreign Secretary asked if the Cabinet Crisis Committee had, in fact, convened before the storming of the jet had taken place. The question was designed to embarrass. He was well aware of the shortfall.

'The Right Honourable Gentleman knows that there was no meeting of the Crisis Committee prior to the storming of the jet,' the Prime Minister replied. 'Time did not permit.'

'This is an example of the preemptive action the TREVI committee advocate?' the Shadow Foreign Secretary asked. 'Five innocent lives lost. Many more seriously injured.'

'The loss of innocent lives is most regrettable, but there was no alternative but to storm the jet . . . .'

A cry of disapproval went up around the House. The Prime Minister continued even more assertively.

'More lives would have been lost had this action not been taken immediately. We had been kept informed of every development from the moment the jet was seized in mid-air. It became clear that the terrorists, one of whom was known to be mentally unstable, could not be reasoned with. They had already committed acts of violence on board the jet before it landed at Barcelona Airport.'

In reference to claims made in the press purportedly based on Foreign Office information, the Prime Minister invoked the principle of confidentiality, and the obligations of staff in the civil service and security services. Disclosures harmful to national security could not be tolerated. There would be an inquiry.

The question was again put to the Prime Minister: were these allegations well-founded?

Such disclosures were invariably a misrepresentation of the facts. That was as much as the Prime Minister would say on the matter.

Again, the debate was drawn to the hijacking.

'Her Majesty's Government sanctioned this *improvised* attack on the jet?'

'It was a planned, coordinated assault on a hijacked British Airways jet. It was a lawful rescue operation of British citizens.'

'There were other nationals on board. Were their governments consulted? Were they even briefed? Were they notified in advance of this assault on the jet? Were our EEC partners kept informed? I would suggest, Prime Minister, that this crisis was managed appallingly.'

'You cannot manage a crisis,' insisted the Prime Minister. 'You respond to each development as it is presented to you with the resources at your immediate disposal. To answer the Right Honourable Gentleman's question: yes, the governments of other nationals on board were kept informed; they *were* notified in advance of the assault; our EEC partners were kept fully aware of events. We all supported the action taken by the Spanish authorities.'

There were sceptical grumblings to be heard throughout the House.

'Why, then, were our own forces not used in the rescue bid?'

'There simply wasn't time. The situation on board the jet had deteriorated such that a critical point had been reached when the jet put down at Barcelona Airport. The terrorists were not interested in negotiating. They had made that abundantly clear. We could not allow the jet to refuel and continue to Beirut Airport, where there could be no hope of controlling the ground in any rescue attempt, where, most likely, the hostages would have been taken from the jet and dispersed in the suburbs of the city, where there could be no hope of rescue. When the jet put down in Barcelona to refuel, a decision had to be taken and acted upon immediately.'

'Was the assault on the jet by the Spanish anti-terrorist squad rehearsed?'

'It was a planned and coordinated operation,' the Prime Minister repeated.

'Was there good intelligence, reconnaissance and rehearsal?'

'Every effort was made to ensure the safety of those held hostage . . . .'

There were more cries of dissatisfaction from the back-benches.

'Intelligence *was* good, but time was pitifully short. It was a brave and successful rescue that saved the lives of one hundred and ten passengers and crew.'

More cries of dissatisfaction.

In the smoking room of the House of Commons prior to the emergency debate, there had been the usual doubts infor-mally expressed as to the effectiveness of the financial con-trol of MI5 and MI6 exercised through the Secret Vote.

'What guarantee have we of efficiency if we may not audit the accounts?'

There were inconsistencies. No one was accusing the security services of corrupt practices, of course, but wasn't there a tendency towards 'natural dishonesty' on the part of the security services?

The handling of the Barcelona operation was commonly described as 'most irregular'. Rumours of a botched MI6 job persisted, and now the Government would have to cover for them. The nation's honour had also been hijacked. The Prime Minister and Foreign Secretary were sure to be over-praised or blamed.

★

The current security alert had been discussed. The thorny subject of visa and immigration control had been exhausted. The debate returned to the issue of preemptive action taken by the security services.

There was no room for complacency, the Prime Minister insisted. The full implementation of the recommendations made by the TREVI committee marked the difference between the committed and the uncommitted for Britain and her EEC partners.

Such a policy heralded political decay, countered the Leader of the Opposition. It ensured that authorised but deniable security operations would be the order of the day.

'Where does it stop?' the Right Honourable Gentleman asked. 'Are we to sanction the kidnapping of families of known terrorists?'

Had C been made accountable in that chamber, his answer to the first question would have been: it stops at the earliest possible stage, depending on information gathered. This would answer the second question also. There was no profit in stating that in the dirty business of international espionage there was nothing particularly dirty about kidnapping. Besides, much of the dirt could be avoided if the firm was well informed.

The preemptive-action issue inevitably led back to the Barcelona hijacking.

'Would the Prime Minister tell us, if the information on the hijacking was exhaustive, how five passengers died and more were injured? I would suggest that the Prime Minister was ill-advised in reaching his decision.' The fact that he had not included the Foreign Secretary in his summing-up was a clear indication that he believed the decision to storm the jet had come from the Prime Minister's lips at the behest of MI6.

'It was not possible to rehearse under the circumstances,' the Prime Minister repeated. 'There is no doubt in my mind that the proper course of action had been taken. The decision to launch the rescue without delay was based on sound intelligence. It was a joint decision taken by myself and the Spanish authorities with the full cognisance and support of the governments of other nationals held hostage. The rescue itself was mounted entirely by Spanish forces. We have them to thank for the one hundred and ten lives saved.'

It was not surprising that the Prime Minister concluded by saying that the adoption of such a stance in the face of international terrorism made a major contribution to international security.

The Leader of the Opposition suggested that the Prime Minister's explanation as to how the decision to storm the jet was 'flimsy, to say the least': parliamentary language for *We don't believe a word of it.*

2

The yellow taxi-lamp mounted on the corner-railing pillar of the House of Commons was flashing. The emergency debate was over. It had run late. Parliament Square had cleared of tourists and commuters. The unseasonal cold snap had taken fierce grip. In a way, it was a convenience, an excuse to hurry to one's destination. In a city expecting bombs, few linger.

The Defence Intelligence Committee was tapping its Cabinet sub-committee foot impatiently, waiting for further news of the expected terrorist attack in Britain. The Defence Intelligence Committee would be the overseer of any pre-emptive action by the security services. Premptive action would have political repercussions. The committee was in the awkward position of being watchdog, advisor and potential scapegoat. Paradoxically, it relied on the security services to furnish in full the information on which it based its judgements.

That same evening, however, the Defence Intelligence Committee met at the request of MI5. Bradshaw attended with marked street and airport maps, photographs and a wad of printed information. Also summoned to the meeting were the head of C13 and a Detective Inspector from Special Branch.

Bradshaw declared matter-of-factly that there had been a breakthrough in intelligence. The security services would shortly be in a position to move against three terrorist cells in, or on their way to, Britain.

The Prime Minister's desire for tough action could hardly have been followed up more rapidly, it would seem.

In Bath, Hinkley studied the weir from a window and listened to Radio 3.

'So, there was absolutely nothing to worry about?'

'Heavens, no.'

It was coming out of C's office. Calkie had cuffed Baxter, but was keeping his own council. He was covering for Klinovec. Hinkley, out of play, was keeping his mouth shut. These factors were linked, Hinkley had decided, but how?

There had been a second call on the blank telephone. An intermediary. Someone in another part of the building willing to dial Hinkley's Chelsea number and put him through. Hinkley knew she'd be there when they telephoned. They wouldn't bother putting a call through to an empty house, and they'd know whether or not Mary was out teaching her Japanese businessman, or with her confessor. She'd run to the priest now that Otis Baxter had gone missing. She'd telephone the Royal Marsden repeatedly. She'd leave her husband to the answering machine. If, as Hinkley had been hoping, his battered brother, Paul, were to ring, he would leave no message on an answering machine.

What was she doing in the house now?

Dressing to visit Geoffrey.

Hinkley took the call. It was as if he had not returned from Barcelona. It was another of those distended, remote calls, a promise exchanged over a great distance that one would never quite desert the other.

In Moscow, there were others who had grown impatient. Nothing the Director or General Malenkov had yet asked, proved threatening, but Vigodskaya was sure he was closing in for the kill.

'And you say you know this man, Jack Hinkley?' Vigodskaya asked.

'I said I know *of* him.'

'You haven't made clear the circumstances of your knowing him.'

'Forgive me, Colonel Vigodskaya, I thought I had made it perfectly clear. I said I know *of* him. He served in Berlin . . . .'

'Yes, we know that,' interrupted Vigodskaya. 'We have the dates.'

'Then you know more about him than I do,' countered Klinovec. 'Until recently I was not aware that he had been posted elsewhere. He didn't interest me then; he doesn't interest me now. While temporarily based in Berlin, as a matter of routine I read the file on him. I recall it was brief, and what there was of it made dull reading.'

'The British have arrested him. He betrays the American, Otis Baxter, then they arrest him too. What do you suppose that means?'

'The British are in a mess. They're finding traitors everywhere. It is most gratifying.'

'We have lost a valuable source in Otis Baxter, and you say we should be gratified?'

'Otis Baxter has long outlived his usefulness. The British have been using him to pass us misleading information.'

'This has not been proved,' interjected Snitkina.

'It is convenient for you to believe so, Major Klinovec,' added Vigodskaya.

Their protests were lame. They both knew Baxter was useless.

'I'm surprised you trust his word, Colonel Vigodskaya,' said Klinovec. 'I am surprised that Major Snitkina does not agree that in removing Otis Baxter, the British are assisting with our great cleansing.'

Klinovec's bitter inference that the purge within the KGB was an excuse for a witch-hunt was very much part of his defence tactics.

Snitkina did not care to comment on Baxter's arrest.

Klinovec had already stated why he had not brought the full story to the attention of the Directorate. He had explained that he had kept his own counsel in order to ensure that Baxter would not hear from Vigodskaya or Snitkina of his long-standing suspicions.

The subject of Hinkley and Baxter had been exhausted.

'The British agent, Larch,' said Snitkina, 'the one who followed you to my apartment in Barcelona . . . are you sure he was alone?'

'Quite sure.'

'He was in radio contact.'

'What does it matter what he said to others on his radio? He was alone. He didn't hinder my passage.'

Vigodskaya fell on his prey from a great height.

'I suggest, Major Klinovec, that before we dealt with him, the British agent had identified you to his colleagues, and that as a result you were confronted in the railway station by British agents, that you were taken away, but then later released because, Major Klinovec, it was an unfortunate mistake on the part of the British. Their Barcelona Station hadn't been told that you were in the pay of MI6.'

'You were seen at the railway station, Major Klinovec,' Snitkina added weightily.

Klinovec answered according to his brief, without hesitation or embellishment. The stiff leg he had had, and the now-fading marks on his throat, were proof of the struggle. The rebuke, in the form of an attack on Vigodskaya's integrity, and Snitkina's by association, momentarily confounded both men.

'Your true purpose in visiting Paris was to rendezvous with a British agent,' insisted Vigodskaya, almost shouting. 'How much do they pay you, Major Klinovec?'

Klinovec's coldness, in contrast to Vigodskaya's belligerence, served to create the impression that Vigodskaya was embarked upon a vendetta.

3

In London, the freak cold snap continued. On the morning of the raids, gas-pipes were bursting in the clay under pavements. The breath expelled through the tightly knitted balaclavas worn by the SAS condensed thickly in the air.

There were to be five raids. Four in the suburbs of London. One at Heathrow Airport. Parliament and public would be impressed. EEC partners would be impressed. Even the Americans would be impressed – politicians and sceptical security services alike. The British press would praise the British security services.

MI5 would have reason to be pleased with a successful operation of this scale. Although it would be C13 supported by the SAS who would coordinate the operation and make the arrests, MI5 would be seen as the body responsible for the intelligence behind the operation. Undoubtedly, the Home Secretary would have been briefed from Curzon Street. It would not dispel allegations that the service was politically naive, but it would show that it could be a politicians' friend, if not saviour.

At the appropriate moment, C, in a private audience with the Prime Minister and Foreign Secretary, would quietly claim credit for the intelligence-gathering abroad that had made the interception of the terrorists possible. He would quote but not identify his souce, and again give solemn warning of the new threat from splinter terrorist groups. Century House, he would insist, needed fresh financial resources before any other of the security services if there were to be effective counter-measures. On being commended by the Prime Minister and Foreign Secretary, C would remind both that in broader terms, the unsung success of MI6 would continue only if the support of the Exchequer was realistic, by which of course he meant, if the budget were to expand progressively.

The three terrorists lost in Tangiers, and subsequently located in Lisbon, had arrived at Heathrow Airport on a flight from Nice. Their two associates – those who had also set out from Damascus – were now lost in Tripoli. Of the two other cells, one was known to have four members, three of whom were long-term sleepers in Britain. The remaining one, plus the other cell – which was known to have four members also – were already based at addresses in Bayswater and West Kensington. They were not all living at those addresses. There were two other houses under surveillance, one in Wandsworth, the other in Lewisham. The information was that they were about to embark on a bombing campaign. It was understood that one, or perhaps two members of each cell would be used only for the planting bombs. The others would operate in supporting roles, providing explosives, reconnaissance, transport, food and safe passage.

The four raids in the city took place at first light. The anti-terrorist squad, supported by the SAS, gained entry to each house by force, and made their arrests. For C, it was the end of a protracted operation that had begun with intelligence picked up by a hostile service in the Middle East. He deplored the use of the SAS in this instance. These were not sieges. It was not a beleaguered jet on the tarmac, as at Barcelona Airport. The presence of so many armed officers gave the impression of a country under threat from terrorism getting lucky, then over-reacting. In the event, his fears were amply borne out, though not specifically as a result of the SAS presence. In the customs and immigration hall of one Heathrow terminal, the three new arrivals were engaged too soon by one over-anxious police officer, who misread the sudden movement of one of them. He left no time between his shouting 'Armed police!' and applying the nine pounds of pressure required to pull the trigger of his revolver. It was a dreadful miscalculation, compounded by the panic which broke out in the restricted area. Uniformed police officers were quickly drafted onto the scene in an attempt to regain control, and reassure the public. The wounded man lay on the floor, twitching. The polished tiles were perfectly level. With each pump of the heart, the pool of blood on the floor grew a little.

The other two were arrested and quickly led to a waiting van, one having to be forcibly taken from the side of his bleeding companion.

In all, eleven arrests were made. No armed resistance had been offered. The fact that not one of them was in possession of a firearm was cause for concern given that one man had been fatally wounded by a police officer's bullet. A large quantity of explosives was seized, together with sophisticated detonators in Bayswater and West Kensington. Forensic tests were carried out at Victoria Road Police Station, where the accused were subsequently held.

Part Six

1

Hinkley read about the arrests in the newspapers Lockwood brought him. Although the press noted the relief in Whitehall and among the public generally, there was not the applause that had been expected. The shooting at the airport had put a different face on things. It was yet another serious incident that called into question the training and deployment of armed police officers. There would be no riots on this occasion. The killing produced a different kind of tension. It renewed fears of terrorist attack. One of the terrorists lay in the city morgue, awaiting a holy burial in the desert. Ten others in Victoria Road Police Station had been charged with conspiring to cause an explosion, or possession of explosives, or both. They were sure to be convicted and imprisoned in Britain.

'Did they get them all?' Hinkley asked.

'Yes, it seems they did,' replied Lockwood. 'And a mound of plastic explosives. Ugly business that shooting, though.'

'It's inexcusable.'

'I was talking with Pickering before I came down here. He had had one of his little tête-à-têtes with Bradshaw in the back of his car. Apparently, one of our lovely boys picked up some information in the Middle East. Wouldn't say where. So they've us to thank for it – not that Bradshaw *did* actually thank us. No fear of that happening.'

'The sly bastard has Pickering in his pocket.'

'Perhaps,' said Lockwood doubtfully. 'Pickering was anxious to know if I knew the source. He didn't come straight out with it, of course. He couldn't be seen to be out of the picture, but I knew what he was after.'

'Well? *Do* you know?'

'Haven't a clue, old boy,' said Lockwood dryly. 'Thought I'd ask you.'

Hinkley wasn't in the mood for Lockwood's wit.

'So this is to be another debriefing?'

'Yes. That's it exactly.'

They were alone in the room. Hinkley stubbed out his cigarette in the ashtray one of his minders had filled to capacity with ash and crushed butts. He began to pace the room heavily.

'Shall we walk?' Lockwood asked. 'I haven't been in Bath for a long time. Let's visit the Costume Museum, shall we? Have you been there?'

'No, I haven't been there,' barked Hinkley.

'Oh, you'll like it. For a moment it puts the *Great* back in *Britain*.'

Hinkley wasn't sure whether or not this was another example of Lockwood's dry wit. He studied his posture, framed as it was in the window. He fixed on the sloping forehead of his peanut-shaped head, which terminated with a right-angled nose above fixed lips. He decided that Lockwood was perfectly serious about the museum.

'Then I'll take you for afternoon tea in the Pump Room,' Lockwood added.

★

Lockwood insisted that they take the guided tour of the costume collection.

'We might both learn something,' he said. The implication was that he might pick up a tit-bit to add to his already substantial knowledge of the subject, and that Hinkley might, if he was attentive, learn the basic distinctions.

Lockwood was politely silent throughout the tour. Hinkley followed the small group with the same heavy footfall begun in his redundant hotel room. He had been giving a lot of thought to the connection between Klinovec, the nefarious Otis Baxter and himself. Now, something Lockwood had said had struck a chord. 'One of our lovely boys' had picked up some information in the Middle East. No one seemed to know who.

'My passion is history,' declared Lockwood as they left the museum.

'What about the faggot in Banking?' asked Hinkley. 'The one with the kip in Bermondsey.' He was goading him.

'That is a *completely* different thing,' said Lockwood dismissively. 'You can be *so* vulgar, Jack. It wouldn't surprise me if you've learnt nothing in the past hour.'

'I've got other things on my mind.'

'You don't realise that what you've seen in there is a measure of security through the ages. The past is always with us. That's a lesson we'd do well to remember.'

'I'm just concerned about the last ten days.'

Hinkley decided to test a theory on Lockwood as they walked the short distance to the Roman Baths.

'Pickering was in the old man's chair the day after the Barcelona hijacking . . . so it was Pickering who recalled me to London?'

'Pickering issued the instructions, yes . . . .'

'It wasn't you?'

'Jack, you know I have complete confidence in your abilities. I've stood by you in this.' Lockwood was again uncomfortable, as though his standing by Hinkley had not been enough. He didn't like Hinkley studying his face. 'Don't sulk,' he snapped. 'It doesn't suit you.'

Hinkley had the answer he was looking for. Pickering *was* in C's chair the following day. Why? Because C was in Paris. Klinovec was on that British Airways flight from Berlin to Paris to meet C.

It made sense.

But why should both men take such a risk?

The answer – though Hinkley was not to know it yet – was that since Steibelt's death there had been no middle-man, no cut-out. There was no one in place and in the pay of MI6 whom Klinovec trusted to replace Steibelt. The mobility Klinovec enjoyed in his capacity as Deputy Head of Directorate S would have to serve as cover until a trustworthy candidate could be found.

C was afraid Klinovec wanted out, that he would ask for asylum. The rendezvous in a Paris suburb had a dual purpose. There was the delivery of the information Klinovec had on the movements and intentions of three terrorist cells. This intelligence, Klinovec had picked up in Damascus through his Soviet sources. The attacks were to take place in London. Klinovec was able to say how and when the terrorists would arrive. He could list those already in London. He had addresses for them in Bayswater, Lewisham, Wandsworth and West Kensington. With such intelligence on offer, there could be no doubt about Klinovec's worth. The other purpose of the meeting was reassurance. C needed to judge if his agent could withstand the pressure placed on him.

It was a supreme irony that the flight Klinovec had boarded in Berlin for Paris should be hijacked by Arab terrorists. It was also a sobering indication of how much intelligence-gathering there was to be done, for neither Moscow Centre nor Century House had had any warning of that hijacking, or of the Paris bomb that followed. It was with this in mind that C had told the Prime Minister of the obscure terrorist factions forming loose alliances, in an attempt to impress upon his political master the gravity of this new threat.

A chamber orchestra was playing in the Pump Room, the elegant tea-room above the spa waters. The place was nearly full, with a mixture of tourists and residents of Bath. Lockwood and Hinkley sat at a table to one side, and ordered afternoon tea for two.

'You'd think with all this hot water bubbling underneath, it would be warm,' announced Lockwood, removing his coat. As always, he was wearing his smart, tailored suit and loud silk tie. He would never sit in a public indoor space without removing his coat, no matter how low the temperature was. 'It's colder here than it is in London.'

'The biscuit factory in Liverpool won't know when to switch from ginger-nuts to ice-cream cones,' said Hinkley sullenly. He wasn't there to talk about the weather.

'You were happy in the sun, weren't you?' asked Lockwood.

'I still am happy in the sun,' came the reply. In light of Hinkley's treatment in London, it was all right to tell a white lie.

Lockwood began to regale him with an anecdote about his time serving in Lisbon, but Hinkley wasn't listening. His eyes were fixed on the musicians, his mind climbing up and down the greasy skeleton of the previous ten days.

At some point, Lockwood stopped. He changed tack. The music resisted the disrupting words Lockwood spoke in a small, even voice, but the words were repeated. Hinkley looked to his host and saw the words come out of his mouth, but didn't take them in.

'What's the matter?' Lockwood asked.

'Nothing,' replied Hinkley distractedly. 'You still haven't told me where I stand.'

When the chamber orchestra had retired, Lockwood finally addressed himself to business.

'Jack, you're out,' he said, pouring tea.

Whatever about Lockwood's ability to offer comfort, he had grace.

'Perhaps not for good. I don't know. I had no part in the decision.'

He could see Hinkley floundering, but he was determined not to soften a hard reality.

'They're calling it a suspension. You'll be paid until they see fit to make it official. I'm sorry.'

2

Hinkley felt as the loyal Zeisler must have done when he was handed back to the East Germans – whereupon he was promptly relieved of his command, and relegated to the task of teaching raw recruits to the Haupt-Verwaltung Aufklarung how to arrange meetings and pass on information on the street.

Suddenly, Hinkley was the introspective onlooker, the solitary one whose ability to analyse his misfortune grew weaker by the minute as information grew steadily colder.

Was he inept, or was it merely the circumstances that allowed him to be so used? Even this question now seemed unanswerable.

Naturally, Hinkley considered the faint promise of re-induction to be nothing more than a fob-off, but equally, he could not see the whole business ending here.

For the moment, he would do nothing but contemplate the events which had been set in motion by the hijacking, repeat his search for listening devices in his house, rock gently in the rickety cradle that was his estranged family. His one contingent act had been to telephone Pilar from a callbox, ostensibly to make arrangements to pay the rent on his apartment, for although the consulate had secured the lease, the rent was paid in cash each month. The landlord was cheating on his tax. He knew the Inspector of Taxes would not ask for a foreign consulate for financial particulars of rented property.

'I haven't got the key,' said Pilar.

'Yes you have. Besides, you don't need it to pay the rent. Just call to the landlord's office with the cash. I'll put a cheque in the post for you today.'

'How long will you be away? You tell me that.'

'Not long. Another week. Maybe a little longer.'

'I won't pay.'

'Please, Pilar.'

'No. You come back and pay it yourself. I'm too busy.'

'I'll be back as soon as I can.'

'I'll still be busy. I've got work to do, you know.'

'Pilar. Please.'

'OK. I pay. I pay.'

'Call by the flat and make sure everything is all right.'

'I told you. I've lost the key.'

'No you haven't. If the cat shows, feed it, will you?'

'I kill the cat.'

Hinkley really just wanted to hear her voice. He didn't know whether or not he love her, this bad-tempered girl his daughter's age, but he missed her. She was the only person with whom he was intimate.

Mary welcomed him as she had done on his return from Barcelona. He was in the house waiting for her. He had just completed another fruitless search for bugs.

'Is that you, Jack?' she called, shutting the hall door. She knew somebody was in. The door was unlocked.

'I'm in here.'

'Sitting in the dark again?' She switched on the lights. He rose to his feet. They pressed cheek to cheek and kissed the air. The perfume meant more to him than the weak embrace.

'How is Geoffrey?'

'The same. We can only pray.'

Mary is praying, thought Hinkley. The priest had put her up to it.

'He doesn't deserve this,' said Mary. Any mention of her brother upset her enormously. The strain of having to cope alone with Geoffrey's illness was evident.

'Do you want a drink?' she asked, with wet eyes.

'Let me get them. What do you want? Vodka? Gin?'

He took her coat from her. He made her sit down. He brought the drink to her.

'I suppose I'm not allowed to ask where you've been?'

'Look, I'm not going back to Barcelona – not for a while, at least. I'll stay as long as you need – until Geoffrey is out of hospital.' The qualification followed immediately. It was no help to either of them.

Mary forced the recovery.

'We've had a card from Vanessa and Roger.'

'Already?' Hinkley was glad of the change of subject, but it didn't go far.

Mary swallowed her drink in one go.

'Will you come with me to the hospital after dinner?'

'You know I will. You don't have to ask.'

'How am I to know what appointment you've made?'

'Let's go out to dinner.'

'There isn't time.'

A compromise was agreed. After he read the postcard from Vanessa and Roger, Hinkley went to get food from the Indian restaurant.

They were late for the hospital anyway. That is to say, they were not among the first to arrive for the restricted evening visit.

Word of Hinkley's indefinite suspension spread quickly among his colleagues at Century House. Although he had spent little time in London in the past two years, to many he was a familiar archangel. No reason for the suspension had been given officially. It was left to 'informed' quarters to provide one. It was believed that there had been a cock-up at Barcelona Airport, a missed opportunity, for which Hinkley was being blamed. Foreign Office talk supported this. There were a few who suspected that Hinkley had been caught out in treacherous dealings in some especially sensitive area. The arrests in Highgate Cemetery, and what was thought to be Hinkley's interrogation in Bath, suggested as much. Chief among Hinkley's defenders were Lockwood and deWitt. Lockwood was in a position to dispel such conjecture, and to do so informally.

Throughout the capital's security community – that was the new term imported from America – there was among the informed, genuine surprise at the suspension, though the matter was overshadowed by the fate of the police officer who had shot the terrorist at Heathrow. He, too, had been suspended – in his case, pending an inquiry. The press were clamouring for details of the security operation that had led to the killing. An internal inquiry was not enough, critics maintained. A full judicial inquiry was needed. Inevitably, it was suggested that the mismanaged security operation had thwarted one terrorist attack only to incite others. References were made to the Barcelona hijacking, to the storming of the jet. Was this mismanagement to be the mark of the new, united response to international terrorism?

In Moscow, the editor of *Pravda* commissioned a follow-up piece to the article the paper had carried two days earlier concerning the arrest of more than thirty Arabs and Arab sympathisers, and the killing of another in London. The second article would expose how sweeping powers afforded to the British secret police were being applied to reassure the British public that enemies fostered by an imperialist past were being delt with. The exercise of such powers would be linked with continued support for American global expansionism.

Moscow Centre had given up waiting for Mikka or anyone else to collect the hired car parked near the stadium. They had taken it into one of their service garages. A preliminary search had revealed nothing of consequence. They had put their forensic department to work. They had found a considerable variety of food particles, most animal-fat-based. This slob must have eaten all his meals in the car, they had said. They had found nothing else.

The car was stripped down. Stuffing was removed. Hollows examined. The engine dismantled. When they were that thorough, they were apt to exchange worn parts in their own car-engines for those in a compatible model on the garage-jack. Hired cars were particularly prized. They were usually well maintained. Having yielded no clues as to Mikka's whereabouts, the car the Czech had hired left the garage much the poorer for its inspection.

The Second Directorate issued a photograph and missing-person's bulletin to KGB officers in Moscow. The Militia were not alerted, nor were the Swiss authorities notified.

★

In Dzerzhinsky Square, the case against Klinovec was dropped. It might even be described as having been disproved. Vigodskaya, with Snitkina's support, had failed to produce anything other than circumstantial evidence against Klinovec. Baxter's failure to extract damning evidence from Hinkley had ensured the collapse of their case. The Director and General Malankov were unimpressed with the circumstantial evidence. The Director's judgement was what mattered, and in this instance he had the support of a General.

Klinovec had succeeded in portraying his accusers as ambitious men with a vindictive streak. His recommendation that Mariya Isayeva and Stepan Andreyev in Paris be replaced, was to be immediately implemented, on the Director's orders. Furthermore, changes made in personnel stationed throughout the Fifth Geographic Department since Major Snitkina had been commissioned, were to be reviewed in the Director's office the following morning.

Major Snitkina would have to defend every decision he had made. As for Colonel Vigodskaya, his integrity had been undermined. His superiors would be unforgiving.

General Malenkov advised that Major Klinovec curtail his unorthodox ventures. Klinovec was duly cautioned by the Director.

Klinovec cast a stony gaze at Vigodskaya, who seemed to be shrinking before his eyes.

Incredibly, Klinovec was to escape with a minor reprimand. It was more than he dared hope for.

3

Some people had a talent for sleeping, for passing out when overburdened with problems. Not Hinkley. He had to walk. He had to do it the hard way. Only physical fatigue would bring that kind of sleep.

In Knightsbridge he met a neighbour, a solicitor with a lucrative practice. Hinkley had come from Hyde Park, the neighbour from Harrod's Food Hall. The neighbour was about to step into a taxi when he saw Hinkley. He offered him a lift. He was anxious that Hinkley accept.

'I say, you didn't see two suspicious characters sitting in a car opposite our house?' he asked, getting straight to the point. 'We've been burgled.'

'No, I'm afraid I didn't. I shall ask Mary.'

'I expect the police will be knocking on your door with routine enquiries. It upset Elizabeth enormously. I've had to send her to her sister's for a spell.' He indicated his food-hall shopping bags, from which Hinkley was meant to deduce that his neighbour was catering for himself in the absence of his wife. 'She's the one who saw them . . . sitting in their car . . . reconnoitring, no doubt.'

'Did they take much?'

'Small valuables, mostly. The kind of things one can put in one's pocket. They rifled the drawers. The invasion of privacy, that's the worst of it,' he said unconvincingly. 'I've had Banham's in, fitting new locks, though I don't imagine it will make much difference. I wouldn't be at all surprised if they came back. I've been down to Chelsea Police Station. We can expect a bobby on the beat. Better than nothing, I suppose.'

'How did they get in?'

'The back garden, the detective says. They climbed the scaffolding – you know, the one against the gable of the last house on the terrace – then they crossed the gardens to *my* house.'

Did Hinkley detect the trace of a boast that his neightbour's house had been chosen above others whose gardens had been crossed?

'Bloody silly leaving scaffolding like that,' the neighbour said. 'I've already complained.'

Hinkley was tired. He found it difficult to be concerned, but when he heard that his neighbour's bi-focal glasses had been wilfully smashed by the burglar, or burglars, he was more sympathetic.

'I found them in pieces on the kitchen floor. Smashed under heel. It was a senseless act.'

Hinkley gave that some thought. No, this wasn't a senseless act. There was a motive. It was an attack on literacy, on the desire to learn from books, to be informed. Somehow, this was the heart of the matter.

The image of the smashed glasses on the floor stayed with him all day. It was the same bitterness that had caused

217

his brother to be beaten. Here was an enemy no security service, no matter how resourceful, could contain. This cancer would only be defeated through education, and in the meantime the marauders beat people and smashed their reading-glasses.

Hinkley called to his brother's flat in Notting Hill. There was no on there. He tried looking through the basement window. The ivy plants had gone from the mantelpiece. Perhaps they had died. He couldn't see much else. The landlady had got her way, or Paul had left the place: the net curtains were again hung.

'Never back there,' Paul had said of Liverpool.

Hinkley rang anyway.

Their mother answered. It was not the time to talk to her. He disguised his voice and asked for Paul. Her children had left her more than twenty years earlier, had scarcely visited her since; she wasn't surprised or puzzled at the enquiry.

No. Paul wasn't there.

The old woman was still a stranger. Hinkley cut her short. Sentimentality disgusted him. She would die soon, and that would be the end of it.

It was dark again when Hinkley returned from a long, solitary walk by the river. When he turned the corner into his lucky street, he felt he had suddenly been caught by the arm in some great barbed hook that ripped his flesh. He had been shot. In spite of the acoustic chamber created by the terraces, there was no report. The bullet had come from a silenced gun. From a high angle, Hinkley thought. From the scaffolding at the end of the terrace, perhaps.

He heard the second shot – or rather, it ricocheting on the railings. It was a hideous twang. He had already dropped to a crouch and rolled clumsily. He kept moving. He ran in a crouch. He put solid cover between himself and what he thought was the gunman's vantage-point.

Two bad shots, Hinkley's racing brain spat. An amateur? Someone with a pistol? They should have waited until he was further from the corner, until he was halfway along the terrace. There would have been more time for the second shot.

He ran into Flood Street. People crossing the junction with King's Road served to give the shooting a ring of unreality, but his arm hurt like hell. Fortunately, the bullet had missed the bone and passed through the flesh of the arm.

No one followed. He didn't expect they would. They would try again another time.

In spite of the bulk of his sleeve, very soon there would be blood everywhere. It was an absurd but entirely pragmatic act. He walked into a chemist on the King's Road. It was about to close. The staff were preoccupied with the end-of-day procedures. Though Hinkley was in a state of shock, it seemed to him ludicrous that he should be standing in this bright light, bleeding from a gunshot wound.

He bought an elastic bandage and anaesthetic, antiseptic throat-spray. He didn't have to reach high or low for them. He found himself following the droplets of blood he had left on the floor on his way in.

He had to stop the blood fast. With difficulty, he dressed his wound in the toilet of a nearby pub. So far as he could tell, there was no major damage. The bullet has passed through skin and fat, and had torn away a piece of muscle. His immediate concern, however, was for veins and arteries, but these appeared to be intact.

He was shaking.

He thought he might faint.

He wanted a stiff drink at the bar, but he didn't dare remain still.

★

Going to ground was like returning to one's childhood when an intimate knowledge of a small territory included a hiding-place fit only for a child.

For the moment, it would be that simple. Hinkley's first thought was to call the Panic Desk and have them bring him in. He thought better of this option. It was a sobering thought that he could not completely rule out the possibility that his assailant operated within, or indeed, had been sent by, the firm.

In spite of the old man's stony silence, his failure to extend a hand, his retreat into his illness, Hinkley still had faith in C. He would go to C. What exactly his approach would be, he had not yet decided. Pickering was still in the old man's chair. That much he knew. He would have to go to Scotland, where C was resting. Though it would be trying and uncomfortable with his wound, he decided to travel in stages by coach. The first leg would be from London to Oxford. He had chosen one of the university services because many passengers travelled alone on those routes. He boarded the bus, not at Victoria Coach Station, but at one of the few suburban stops it made before leaving the city. He was dressed for a cold London night. The bullet-hole in his new coat was curiously small. Blood had soaked the lining of the sleeve before he had been able to apply the bandage, but had not penetrated the thick tweed. He feared the effects of fever brought on by his wound. The bus was almost full. He had hoped for a double-seat to himself, preferably at the back of the bus, but he was forced to share. Everything had happened so fast. Now, he would have to sit still and endure the pain.

The bus was delayed. It took more than two hours. In the terminus waiting-room at Oxford, a sort of zoo pavilion, he examined the timetables posted in cases on the walls. He found that he was too late to catch a second bus, which would take him further north. He thought of staying the night at the Randolph Hotel, or the Royal Oxford, or perhaps a smaller establishment. He decided to sleep rough. The police may have been asked to watch for him. A man registering in a hotel alone and without luggage of any kind would cause suspicion. It was too late to purchase a grip-bag or suitcase.

He went looking for a newsagent's. He bought three newspapers and a packet of biscuits.

He left the streets and crossed Christ Church Meadow to the river. He chose a spot in the lea of a boathouse. He attended to his wound. It was more difficult than before. His arm and shoulder were stiff, and the pain was worse. This effectively ruled out his breaking into one of the secure boathouses for shelter.

He padded himself as best he could with wadded news-print. It would be enough to preserve his body-temperature.

For some time, Hinkley was watched by a vixen that had frozen in mid-trot. She seemed to sense that it was a wounded animal that was huddled against the wall. He was glad of its company. He laid out biscuits for her, but she kept her distance. The Oxford foxes moved and fed virtually unimpeded. This vixen didn't need broken biscuits. Unlike her counterpart in London – scrawnier, more tenacious ani-mals, many of which travelled eight or ten miles along dis-used railway tracks each night to feed on chip-papers and Kentucky Fried Chicken bones – she could pick and choose. The Oxford foxes merely crossed surrounding meadows and passed along secluded paths and cloisters to the bins and the hand-outs, to the roast meat, the congealed gravy, the cold potatoes. Hinkley used to watch them at night, spotting them with a torch from his window. In those days, he had an appetite for observing anything he thought oth-ers might miss. Mary fell into that category, along with the foxes. When he moved to London and secured a junior post with MI6, the foxes were replaced by a bird of prey. He had observed it from the upper floors of Century House, return-ing to its nest bearing sparrows hunted over the city. He had thought it might be a peregrine falcon. Peregrines had been introduced to the city of London to control the pigeon and sparrow populations. He eventually found someone in the building who could identify his bird. It was a kestrel, not a falcon. He had made it his business to be curious. There was no such thing as being naturally observant. You had to work at it. He had got lazy in Barcelona. He tolerated the cat because it provided a lesson in laziness.

Once again, Hinkley was watching the wildlife, but it was no longer reassuring. He was too afraid of misreading what was before his eyes.

Suddenly, the vixen was gone. It had crossed the foot-bridge and was skirting the meadow. The wounded animal had smelt of danger.

It was a long, cold night. Hinkley got little sleep. The newsprint became damp with fever-sweat.

In the morning, he crossed the footbridge, followed the tow-path to the botanic gardens, then crossed the street to Magdalen College. Although the chapel did not open to the public until the afternoon, the door was unlocked. Private worship had always been accommodated.

Hinkley had an hour and a half to wait for his bus. He had used all the antiseptic throat-spray on his wound. It had kept the wound free of infection, but the pain was worse than ever. He sat in the quiet and warmth for as long as he could bear, then he took to pacing, then he read the cards that had been posted. *Pray for me. Twenty-three with cancer.* That was the first. The second read: *Pray for me is a girl who travel alone in this dangerous land.*

He read no further.

He chose a long route to the bus station. He needed time to get the ticket transaction clear in his feverish head. London, Mary, the house in Lucky Street, were out of focus. Everything that lay behind was out of focus. A bullet can do that.

4

The river slowed passing through this upland valley. The exposed road kept to one side of the plane before cutting to the river-crossing. A humpback bridge led to the small village, pressed against coppice, mountain and sky. It had never been a poor village. The street was dominated by one large, well-kept country house, its granite window-blocks painted, its walls covered with creeper. Two other such houses – one a rectory – were set back off the road at the end of mossy drives. Hinkley made his way to the rectory.

The village was quiet, engulfed in the kind of peace that is broken by a stranger on foot. Hinkley walked the rectory drive until he came upon decaying cast-iron gates, which were locked with a padlock and chain coated in blue plastic. The padlock was on the inside. Hinkley turned back. He went to the village post office, which was also a grocery shop and newsagent's. He was greeted guardedly. No enquiry would sound innocent to this woman.

'I have a message for Malcolm Pringle,' said Hinkley. 'Could I leave it with you?'

'You could.'

'Could I ask you for an envelope?'

'An envelope . . .' She broke her steady gaze to get him an envelope.

'Thank you. Do I owe you anything?'

'No.'

'I did call to the house, but the gates were locked. When will he get this? It is rather important, you see.'

Turning to one side, he took from his pocket the wrapper the elastic bandage had come in, folded it blank side out, and sealed it in the envelope. It was the only piece of paper he had on his person.

'He'll have it this evening,' the woman said.

'Thank you,' said Hinkley, writing C's surname on the envelope and handing it to her. 'You're so kind.'

He had got the confirmation he had sought. C was at home – or would be by this evening.

Hinkley bought a newspaper and a packet of cigarettes, and left the shop. The village rang with his footsteps. He returned to the rectory grounds, this time avoiding the driveway. The peaty river flowed by the rectory. A good view of house and road could be had from the river-bank close to the bridge.

It was not like the city, where he understood the movement of his fellows, the solid and opaque surfaces, artificial levels, where he might move in plain view and leave no trace. His chosen vantage-point on the river-bank was a thicket beneath a peculiarly shaped tree that appeared to have crashed headlong into the earth. It was a quiet stretch of river. Flat water. That would help. In the countryside, it was a matter of crude camouflage, not calculated deception. Hinkley had been taught the principles of concealment in the countryside at the nursery in Cornwall, but he had never grasped the niceties. Once he had taken up his position in the thicket, he was reluctant to move. The humpback bridge had become a ring with which to peel back the landscape to reveal some featureless and inhospitable place where men trembled like dogs in thunder.

His wound was bleeding again. The blood wouldn't clot. He split open several cigarettes and pressed the tobacco on the wound. Tobacco would encourage the flesh to close, and scar-tissue to form.

As a child in Liverpool, he believed that the clouds were made in the countryside, that they came up out of the ground, rolled up the sky and burst over the city when they snagged on each other. Now it seemed not such a preposterous theory, for there was a mist gathering in the distance across the plane. The clouds above him were low and fast-moving, like smokey gas.

Hinkley felt the panic in his blood. He wanted out of the whole dirty business. Really out. Out of the service. He knew there could be no unlearning. No discarding of skills. Patient Jack Hinkley had excelled at exploiting doubt in others. He had also learnt to mistrust his own fortune, because others, too, had learnt to exploit doubt.

He was glad of the coat Mary had given him. She had always provided support in the most unwitting way.

The prevailing wind, though cold, kept the mist away. Hinkley could watch the house. He watched it for an hour or more. He had established that there were two Special Branch men in a car parked just out of sight of the main gates. There was some farm activity, particularly around the stables, which were a relatively recent addition to the rectory. So far as he could tell, there was no electronic surveillance system installed in the grounds. Satisfied that he could advance some three hundred yards safely, he moved to the tree-line on the edge of the ancient meadow in front of the house. The light was such that he could make out something of the interior. He could follow movements at the front of the house. He could now see the old man tending some potted plants in the conservatory at the east end of the house. He was in thick overalls, a relic of the 1940s: what used to be called a 'siren suit'. Even from a distance, it made him appear unnaturally pale. Out of his city clothes, the old man looked terribly frail. The stiffness of the overalls seemed to keep him standing.

Hinkley had decided that his approach to C should be direct. He would keep his right hand in his pocket and ask for the truth.

In the event, his plan was modified. He did not cross the meadow on his own feet. A heavy blow from an open hand knocked him unconscious. He had no warning of it. It fell from behind.

It was still light when he became conscious. He found himself in a comfortable bed. He was in a room with a low ceiling. There was a dormer window. It was the attic-room of the rectory. His arm-wound had been properly dressed.

It was considerably less painful than before, but he had a thumping headache.

'*I'm* here for the good of my health,' said C. He was standing by the window, backed by a strong evening sun. He was out of his siren suit. He was dressed like a country gentleman now. 'I'm having to rest. My former doctor was indiscreet. This one is inconsiderate. What are *you* doing here?'

Hinkley was still virtually senseless. He offered no immediate reply.

C continued. 'I got the new fellow up here to have a look at you. He says that's a gunshot-wound. Let's you and I talk, shall we? Do you think you can get up?'

C's bodyguard descended the staircase behind Hinkley. *It was him*, thought Hinkley. *You need a hand like his and his thin lips to deliver that kind of blow. Another Davis.*

In the study, the old man grumbled about the temperature of the tea to the housekeeper while he continued to study Hinkley.

'It used to be that he wanted the pot heated,' said the housekeeper. 'Now it's the cups as well.'

'Yes, that's very interesting, Mrs Hedges,' said C. 'Thank you.' He waited for her to leave. In the hall, C's man stepped aside to let her pass.

The old man arranged the tea-things. He took his time sitting down.

'I'm listening,' he said, as though he was suddenly running out of patience.

'You know who tried to kill me,' said Hinkley. 'If you don't know who, you know why.'

C's concern at Hinkley being shot was real, but it went beyond the attack on the man. Hinkley could see that. This shooting had a profound effect on some dreadful scheme.

Hinkley couldn't sit still. He was now standing in the window. He had seen movement across the meadow in front of the house.

'Were you followed?' C asked.

'I don't think so.' He turned to C. There were people clearly visible at the distant tree-line.

'You needn't be alarmed. We keep horses. On weekends we have handicapped children down for riding lessons. Street brats, too. From Glasgow, mostly.' His phrasing and his tone were deliberately provocative. It would make Hinkley more impatient. It would drive him on. They would get to the point sooner. 'We are adequately protected. We won't be disturbed.'

Hinkley was grinding his teeth without realising it. 'So I know Klinovec is our man,' he said. 'There's more to it. Something that's got me shot. Something you're keeping from me. Lockwood says I'm out. That's just what I want. Out. Out of this stinking service. But I'm not out, am I?'

C did not answer immediately. He attended to the tea.

'How do you know *I* didn't send the gentleman with the gun?' he asked, dropping two lumps of sugar into his cup. 'Sugar?' he added.

'Because I'm alive.'

Hinkley wanted to spring on the old man, to catch him by the throat as Davis would have done, to squeeze the truth out of him.

C took Hinkley's reply as a cheap compliment. In the absence of a reply to his second question, he proceeded to sugar Hinkley's tea.

'Tell me about this attempt on your life.'

The old man's brain seemed to be sorting through a hundred permutations.

Hinkley described the shooting incident in Chelsea.

C listened attentively.

'You assume they were not professionals?' said C.

'I was an easy target. An empty street. A clear shot at close range. Even with a pistol, it should have been a kill. They fired two shots prematurely.'

'They were pistol-shots?'

'It would be a fool who used a pistol for sniping, but I can't be sure.'

'You damn well ought to be!' barked C.

The botched shooting seemed to confirm some notion C had been nurturing. It excited him. He was intent on pursuing one track to its end. In contrast, Hinkley had lost sight of his own place in the intrigue. He had looked to the sea of worms he had crossed, and found no trace of his passage. Was the practical Christian too busy scheming with the butcher to shepherd a stray, belonging to his flock?

Suddenly, the old man softened. He distracted Hinkley.

'You see these?' he said, fingering one of a large collection of Chinese snuff-bottles. Their glass was painted on the inside. The fine lines and vivid colours depicted hunting and court scenes, and dragons plying between heaven and earth. 'Marvellous, aren't they?' He insisted Hinkley examine the one he held. 'As you can see, I collect them.

At some point, somebody thought of painting them on the inside. Suddenly, everybody wanted their snuff-bottle to be painted on the inside. Those who had been painting and lacquering on the outside had to adapt or go out of business. They adapted. And these are the results.' He indicated his collection. 'We at Century House have to adapt. We have to change, even though we appear to be doing nicely. We change for the benefit of us all. It can be a dirty business, changing. I have to preside over it. Sometimes I must undertake work by myself. For a man in my position, it's rather like being president of the Euthanasia Society. You become increasingly unpopular as you grow older.'

The old man returned the snuff-bottle to the cabinet. He again turned to address Hinkley.

'When I took office, I resolved never to keep unnecessary secrets. You know about Klinovec. Distasteful though it may be to you, I will tell you his story . . . .'

C had had Lockwood telephone Mary. Good old Lockwood, never unwittingly indiscreet, had again reassured Mary that her husband's disappearance was perfectly in order.

C was anxious to conclude this interview. He wanted to return to London as soon as possible. He didn't ask Hinkley if he was up to the journey. He assumed he was able. They talked in the car on the way to the airport, and on the plane. Both men were candid.

Hinkley wanted to know the extent of MI5's involvement in the affair. Was the house in Chelsea bugged solely because Otis Baxter was sleeping with his wife?

No. It was important to create the impression that Hinkley was the primary target for the eavesdroppers.

For whose benefit was this ruse employed?

For the benefit of Moscow Centre.

To what end?

To cover Klinovec.

C related the contingency plan he had implemented when suspicion fell on Klinovec in Moscow as a result of his remarkable escape from Barcelona.

Had London ordered the assault on the jet knowing Klinovec was on board . . . *because* Klinovec was on board?

That was none of Hinkley's business. It was sufficient to say that Hinkley had performed his duty. It was unfortunate that he had complicated the matter with the kidnapping. It was most regrettable that Larch had lost his life needlessly.

What bearing had Klinovec's clandestine journey to Paris on subsequent events?

C confirmed that he had met Klinovec in Paris. This in itself was final confirmation that C was running Klinovec himself.

It was Klinovec who had procured the intelligence through Soviet sources in Damascus concerning the bombing campaign that was to be conducted in London. C explained that in the absence of the cut-out – Steibelt – Klinovec had delivered the intelligence himself.

So where did Hinkley fit in once he had returned to London? Why the waiting?

C had already answered this, but he recapped. It was a lot for Hinkley to absorb.

'You understand that I had to protect Klinovec. To put it plainly, your services were expendable; his were not. We made it clear that we suspected you of being one of theirs. That you let him go. They're feeling very smug. For what it's worth, you have served our interests well.'

What was to be Hinkley's fate?

Indefinite suspension. Unsung hero on full pay. Not in, not out.

5

In London, Hinkley found that he had a new set of minders. They weren't like the last ones. They weren't always on his tail. They made periodic checks. Like they did on the Soviets in the city. They certainly were no screen against an assassin's bullet. They still believed that Jack Hinkley was a rotten one. MI5 would have been briefed to that effect. C would have seen to that personally. If the bugs in the Chelsea house had not been replaced when Bradshaw's lot came to remove the first batch, there was sure to be a new batch installed. Even Lockwood, deWitt and the others, while defending Hinkley's record in his absence, would privately harbour some doubt. It was, it seemed, a fait accompli.

Even Mary's vain and frightened priest was more in charge of his own destiny than Hinkley of his. Farmer Geoffrey, dying of cancer in the Royal Marsden, had a brighter future.

Such is the unpredictability of human resilience that the seemingly inevitable did not happen – not in the sequence envisaged, that is. The early-morning telephone call that brought news of a death came not from the Royal Marsden, but from Richmond. It was Lockwood calling from his home. C had died at his desk in Century House. It was less than a week since Hinkley had been with him in Scotland. The old man wasn't to have the retirement present he had wanted – namely, an opportunity to examine the file that had been kept on him.

Lockwood said he wasn't surprised at the old man defying his doctor, but he had expected him to slump in the clubhouse at Lord's; England's last batsman would have just been stumped for a duck. He would have wanted to die on his own time – alone, if possible. That's how Lockwood saw it. As it happened, C had been working alone in his office late that night when he suffered the fatal heart-attack.

'Pickering was quick off the mark,' said Lockwood. 'He didn't know whether to call the undertaker or the decorator first. Perhaps now we'll get the net curtains cleaned.'

Lockwood was upset. He was talking too much.

The news of C's untimely death was yet another blow to Hinkley. The only person to know the whole truth of the Klinovec affair was dead. What provision had the old man made in the event of his death? Lockwood told him that Pickering had instructed him to summon Hinkley to a meeting at Century House. Perhaps the answer to Hinkley's unasked question would be given at that meeting.

The meeting with Pickering was a short one. Lockwood was present in his capacity as officer in charge of the Iberian Desk. Pickering ordered Hinkley back to Barcelona. Jeffers would be returning to Madrid, he told him. Hinkley was to pick up where he had left off. There was particular concern about the two terrorists who had gone to ground in Tripoli. There was reliable information suggesting that both were now in northern Spain. The tracking of these and other suspect terrorists had top priority.

In addition, the systematic assessment of new members of the KGB and satellite services operating in Barcelona undertaken by Jeffers in Hinkley's absence was to be completed.

It was to be business as usual. That was what they were saying. Keep your torn arm free of infection, otherwise forget about it. We'll look into the matter in your absence. We'll protect your back. It was to be as though the Klinovec affair had never happened. It didn't mean that Hinkley was free of suspicion. On the contrary. Pickering probably thought it safer to keep him in the field, where, ultimately, it would be easier to catch him out, or to use him as he saw fit. Pickering would want value for the taxpayer's money.

Hinkley was smart enough not to construe this as rehabilitation. However, he recognised that it was better than the limbo in which he currently existed. London had been a nightmare. He would think more clearly sitting on the fire-escape of his apartment-building in Barcelona.

Hinkley accompanied Mary to the Royal Marsden Hospital. Geoffrey was no better, no worse. They hadn't put him on a self-administered morphine-injector. There was still hope.

Geoffrey was happy to see his sister and brother-in-law. They belonged together, his sister and her diplomat husband. They looked out for each other. Geoffrey knew that from talking to each of them separately. He was more worried about the farm. The poultry would have to go. They were too much trouble.

Hinkley told Geoffrey he'd be returning to Spain the following night. Geoffrey would have to come and visit him.

'Let the farm go to pot altogether?' Geoffrey said. 'I just might, Jack!'

Mary had been quiet since Jack had told her he was going back to Barcelona. She wanted to know when he'd be in London again, but she knew there was no point in asking. He wanted to be able to tell her that he would be returning regularly to visit her, but these would be business trips, and she'd know it.

Much of the last day, Jack and Mary spent together. It stretched hideously out of proportion. Loyalty, resilience, regret, united to cause both pain. They had breakfast together. They had lunch together. They performed for each other. It was that kind of closeness.

Late that afternoon, Hinkley took a taxi to his tailor's, where he collected and paid for his new suit.

Mary watched him pack. She felt it was her duty. She had arranged to take her class later than scheduled.

Hinkley had already folded as compactly as he could the coat she had given him.

'That was for London,' she said when she saw the folded garment in the case. 'You'll hardly need it there.'

'It can get very cold,' he said.

Of course he didn't need it. He had packed it because he didn't want her noticing that it was soiled. Dry-cleaning had not completely removed the blood-stain from the sleeve-lining, and the small entrance and exit tears had not been repaired. It was a rum truth that Mary might never know of the wound. She might never see the scar.

His suitcase – the one she had bought him – was already loaded to capacity with the addition of his new suit and Davis's shoes.

'I haven't seen you in brown shoes before,' she said.

'They're new. I don't like them, actually.'

'Do you want some shirts from your drawer?' she asked.

These were part of his London wardrobe that somehow never got worn. White poplin shirts. A ransom of sorts.

'No. I'll be needing them here.'

'You'll telephone . . . ?' she asked. 'For news of Geoffrey,' she added.

'Of course I will. I'm sorry I can't be here for Vanessa and Roger when they return. You'll tell them I've been called away?'

After a hastily arranged wedding, Vanessa and Roger had taken a month's honeymoon. Roger had a lot of pocket-money, Vanessa an exceptionally generous employer. The relationship was doomed to fail. So Hinkley thought.

'I'll tell them,' said Mary.

'If Paul rings, you'll give him my number? Tell him to call me?'

'Yes.'

'If there's anything he needs . . . money, perhaps . . . .'

'Yes,' interrupted Mary. 'I'll see to it.'

'Until I get back.'

Mary nodded.

'Well then . . . .'

Hinkley and his small, overloaded suitcase made their way to the airport. Even allowing for the security alert, he was unnecessarily early for his flight to Barcelona. He had nearly three hours to wait.

On the jet flying south, Hinkley read of the release of the men arrested at Heathrow. The Attorney General had personally reviewed each case to be presented by the Crown. It was decided that the evidence could only be described as circumstantial, except in the case of the dead man, whose suitcase had contained explosives and who bore traces of the same on his person. The forensic evidence gathered at Victoria Road Police Station was inconclusive. All those arrested were to be deported for possessing bogus passports or for having obtained visas under false pretences. The whole truth was more disturbing. There had deliberately been no mention of the explosives-find in London itself. So far as the press and public knew, the three at Heathrow were the bombers. The other arrests in the city were a precautionary measure: political activists or trouble-makers brought in for questioning and found to be aliens without proper visas.

Loudest among the Attorney General's critics was Lord Peacher. The efforts of the terrorist had been frustrated, the killing and maiming of innocent people forestalled, but was this not yet another example of gross incompetence on the part of our security services, he asked. Was Whitehall not empowering the terrorist by pretending to itself and others that it had taken expedient action? Far from discouraging the terrorist, these releases would encourage the fanatic to hold the British people to ransom, he claimed. It made a farce of the TREVI meeting, he insisted.

Hinkley folded his newspaper.

He thought about Klinovec, the one who had risked his life to bring the news of the bombers and made their interception possible. How would he feel, Hinkley wondered, if he knew that in risking his life, all he had secured was a few more nights free from the grief terrorists brought? He wondered if this man, who had brought him so much torment, had a wife and children. If so, was his wife having an affair with a party official? Did he fear for his children's safety in an increasingly unstable world? Did he, too, think he was special in a sour sort of way? Betrayal was never honourable. How well did this juju-man cope with it?

Part Seven

1

A black city skyline. Behind that, ink dragon clouds. Behind them, an electric blue sky. The ground was cold underfoot. The sun-ball hadn't surfaced. The Montjuïc cable swayed in the wind. When that wind dropped and the sun was up, it was sure to be hot.

Barcelona promised to be easier than London. It had been so in the past: would it not continue? It was home-ground for Hinkley. Less could happen without his knowing about it.

The taxi-driver drove at breakneck speed from the airport to Hinkley's apartment in the north of the city. For Hinkley, the fast ride was reassuring.

He left his suitcase in the living room. He had a shower. He brushed his teeth. He shaved. He made iced tea. In the kitchen, he noticed stale cat-food on a saucer on the floor. Presumably, Pilar had put food out for the animal, but it hadn't eaten it, or hadn't come back after a previous feed. There was no rude message from the landlord. Pilar must have paid the rent, as she had promised.

He wanted a long siesta, but he wasn't prepared to lie down just yet. He didn't want to have to conduct a search to confirm that bugs had been installed – not before he had unpacked his suitcase, and he didn't feel like unpacking.

He was expected to confirm his arrival. He rang the consulate. Davis answered. What had C told Davis and Higgins, Hinkley wondered. After all, they knew about the kidnapping and subsequent release of Klinovec. Whatever edited version of the intricate story C had given them, he would have ensured that the precious boxes in which he kept operatives remained insulated from each other, and that Davis and Higgins would not have the opportunity – given that they had the initiative – to check the version which had been given to them. What Hinkley could safely assume was that Lockwood had, on orders from Pickering, briefed the Barcelona Station as to Jack Hinkley's unreliability.

'Welcome back,' said Davis warmly. It was a most un-Davis-like warmth.

'I've got your shoes,' grumbled Hinkley.

After the telephone call, Hinkley put on his new suit and went out for a walk. Inevitably, his walk terminated at his favourite bar near the bird-market.

He hadn't brought Pilar anything. His thoughtlessness kept him prisoner in the bar for nearly two hours. When he did call on her, she was delighted to see him. She told him he was interrupting her reading a novel, but he could stay if he wanted.

'This suit is not right for the weather,' she said, with a cursory pull at the lapel.

Pilar didn't give a damn about a present. Hinkley ought to have known she wouldn't, but he should have got her something anyway.

He was relieved to find her alone.

He was to have a shower while she finished a chapter, she said. Then they'd go to bed.

Pilar was shocked to see his wound. It was healing well, but it still looked nasty: she insisted that he remove the bandage so that she could inspect it; not because she had any medical skills, for she had none – she just hadn't seen a gunshot-wound before. He told her he had sustained it while on a farm in Scotland. It had been a stupid hunting accident.

She got angry with him.

'You bloody Englishman. You want me to say: "Poor Jack"? You want me to organise bullfight? Eh? Eh? You always saying bullfight is disgusting. Now you shoot yourself after birds.' The rest was in Catalan.

Hinkley had to laugh.

She slapped his face hard.

An hour later, she was cutting his hair, naked but for the scissors. She cut it close. It was hot outside. It amused Hinkley to think that she would have cut out Baxter's tongue with her scissors for calling her a fancy-woman.

In the street, Hinkley felt the warm air play on the back of his ears and his exposed neck. It made him feel conspicuous, but for the moment he believed he was safe.

2

Jeffers had thrown a lot out. It was more like an office now. It was too much like an office. It was called an office, but it was meant to resemble a businessman's town apartment. The plants would have to be replaced. The rugs, the soft chair covers, the alcohol would have to be put back. Hinkley noted that the air-conditioning no longer made a racket. Jeffers' occupancy had not been a complete waste.

Hinkley watched the Montjuïc cable-car from the window while Jeffers briefed him on his own good deeds. Davis, the well-dressed thug, put his feet on the desk and kept silent throughout. It was very cosy. Hinkley didn't mind interrupting the monologue. Where was Higgins, he wanted to know.

Higgins had never got used to the food and the climate. He had got his wish. He had been transferred to London.

'He wasn't happy with us,' was how Jeffers put it.

Jeffers was a Foreign Office man at heart.

The new man, and the one replacing Larch, hadn't been invited to this meeting. He was out running errands.

'We've had our hands full with Russians changing staff,' whined Jeffers. 'Finding a replacement for Higgins wasn't easy.' The implication was that Jeffers had been doing some spring-cleaning of his own – that he was a good judge of character and skills, and Hinkley was not.

Hinkley wasn't feeling particularly benevolent.

'Fuck off back to Madrid, Jeffers. I know what I've to do.'

★

Hinkley could find no bugs in his apartment. Each successive search was no more reassuring than the last.

The cat had come back. Hinkley and the cat spent two or three hours of each cool evening sitting out on the fire-escape. There wasn't much of a view from that side of the building, but he could watch television through the open window when he got weary of casting each of his colleagues at Century House in the most disturbing scenario he could create by twisting the facts available to him.

Maybe, after all, he and Klinovec had muddled through. No amount of twisting, it seemed, could produce a feasible answer to the question of who had shot at him, and with what motive.

They were working hard at the Barcelona Station. Hinkley, in particular, had a lot of work to do. There was something odd about the turnaround of KGB staff in the city. He had to find out why a number of those who had been shipped back to Moscow had suddenly surfaced again in Barcelona. As for locating the terrorists in transit, there had as yet been no further information, no sightings.

★

Hinkley and guest were invited to a small dinner party on Xavier's yacht. Pilar said she didn't want to go, but she dressed elegantly and accompanied Hinkley. She reluctantly admitted that she liked his new suit and that it was appropriate dress for the occasion.

Even Miguel was dressed smartly – on bosses' orders. His cigarette seemed to spark between his lips as he piloted the launch into the breeze at full throttle.

Hinkley and his guest were warmly welcomed by their hosts, Xavier and Maria. It was a lavish spread for just a few people.

'You know Jack Hinkley,' boomed Xavier, addressing the two Foreign Office officials Hinkley had snubbed at Barcelona Airport when he and Higgins were chasing Klinovec. 'He's one of your spies.'

'Well, well, Jack Hinkley,' said one in a sweet tone that suggested there was no sordid detail he didn't know about the man standing in front of him. 'Yes, Xavier, we know Jack, but he has to pretend not to know us.' He laughed. He then had the gall to greet Pilar with a kiss.

'How was London, Jack?' Maria asked.

'Cold.'

★

A fortnight after his return to Barcelona, Hinkley was tempted to think that the danger had passed. His scar was a concrete reminder that C had, of course, not told him the whole Klinovec story, and that the danger persisted so long as Hinkley remained uninformed.

Suddenly, he wanted to be with Mary. He telephoned her that night from a public phone.

She talked incessantly about Geoffrey. The news was good. Against all odds, he was recovering. Mary said she'd be spending more time with Geoffrey in Cheshire. She was more married to Geoffrey than to Jack. Mary's wavering faith in God, in prayer, had been restored. She was grateful to Father Peter. There was a postcard to Jack on the hall table. It was from Otis Baxter. It read '*Touché*' and was signed 'Otis'. There was nothing more. The picture showed the White House, and it was postmarked 'Washington, DC'.

Jack didn't seem to care much about Otis Baxter, or Geoffrey, which was far from the truth. He asked if Mary had contacted the locksmith.

No. She hadn't.

He insisted that she call Banham's in the morning to arrange the fitting of a London bar and hinge-bolts.

She questioned the necessity of it.

'Just do it!' he snapped.

His aggressive tone brought the conversation to an end.

3

In Leipzig, Steibelt's widow learnt that her pension was to be increased by six marks per week.

In Moscow, Klinovec was painting his apartment. It would turn out that it was wasted effort on his part. He was to be promoted. He would be getting Vigodskaya's job. He'd be moving to a better apartment. Vigodskaya, with the help of Major Snitkina, had fallen victim to the purge they had been charged with orchestrating. Snitkina, the Americans were pleased to hear, had also been discredited. Word would soon filter through to Century House. The analysts would be able to explain the confusion over the shuffling of KGB staff in the Fifth Geographic Department. Barcelona Station would have one less headache.

In Zurich, the police had got no further with their missing-person's investigation. It was not surprising. The sewage under Moscow now passed freely through Mikka's rib cage.

In London, Larch's widow received the lump-sum payment stipulated in the life-insurance policy her husband had held. On a wet morning, Lockwood supervised the removal of C's possessions from his rented flat in the city. The family would be keeping the house in Scotland. The children's riding lessons would continue uninterrupted.

At Century House, Pickering, the crank, had been confirmed as the new C. He had trimmed his moustache for his meeting with the Prime Minister. Lockwood was to leave the Iberian Desk to be C's deputy.

Roger and Vanessa, returned from their extended honeymoon, had their first major quarrel. Vanessa was spending the weekend without Roger. She and her mother were visiting Geoffrey in Cheshire.

Hinkley's brother, Paul, had had his teeth fixed and was once again taking pornographic photographs in a dingy studio in Soho.

In Washington, Baxter's preliminary interrogation had come to an end. He was to be transferred to a secure establishment in Georgia. They were feeding him well. He was 'singing like a bird', as his chief interviewer put it. They never did discover how the sly dog put a card in the post to Hinkley, though they had learnt he had done so.

Throughout Europe, the security alert persisted. None of the supposed terrorists who had gone to ground in Europe had surfaced. The third missing suitcase-bomb had yet to be found.

In Barcelona, the atmosphere was again sultry. Hinkley couldn't sleep. He paced the floor incessantly. He opened the French windows to the balcony to extend his track. The damn cat yowled to be fed. It watched him as the fox had watched him at the boathouse in Oxford. How could it stand the heat with all that fur?

Hinkley went into the kitchen and made iced tea. The animal rubbed at his legs. He picked up the saucer and reached for an unopened carton of milk. He inadvertently dropped the carton. It remained intact, but a tiny spurt of milk left its mark on the polished floor. Were it not for it catching the light, Hinkley would not have noticed it. He examined the carton closely. He squeezed it. He had to squeeze it hard for it to emit the liquid. The carton had been pierced with a hypodermic needle.

He opened the carton and poured milk into the saucer. He put the saucer on the floor. The cat lapped it up. The drug took effect rapidly. The animal suffered a massive heart-attack. Hinkley's insides churned. The Klinovec affair wasn't over.

They weren't particularly smart bastards. They were just going by the book. Hinkley, a middle-aged diplomat with a heavy workload, was the right material for a heart-attack. They drug they had used would be undetectable in a post-mortem examination. It would have been a clean, quiet, safe kill.

Perhaps other food and liquids had also been injected with the lethal drug. When and where could they have injected the carton? He had bought it that morning in the supermarket. Had they done it in the supermarket? He had spent time out of the apartment. Had they been in his apartment? They'd be outside now, waiting.

Who, and why? Did not these questions share a common answer with the other unanswered question: why had C not confided in his deputy, Pickering, or Lockwood, the veteran on the Iberian Desk? The only conclusion that could be drawn was that he could not trust his senior officers because he believed one had been turned.

If that were the case, it meant that at Hinkley's interrogation in Pickering's flat, either Pickering or Lockwood had knowingly and deliberately betrayed a fellow Soviet agent to protect himself. That the security services had again been infiltrated was a shock. That the shortlist comprised of Pickering and Lockwood was startling. That a man had betrayed another to protect himself and his position was no surprise.

So why dispose of Jack Hinkley? It could only be that Moscow's man believed, correctly, that C was on to him, mistakenly, that Hinkley was his private mole-catcher operating outside Century House, the only other person to know of the hunt until all the senior staff could be cleared of suspicion.

A balance had to be struck. Makeweights, like Jack Hinkley, used to good effect. Moscow Centre had its mole inside MI6, and London had theirs in Moscow. Each side believed that they had the advantage. Neither side would admit to their respective political masters that this supposed superiority was in their favour, for to do so would be to signal contentment. Only Hinkley, it seemed, knew of the traitor in London – though with Klinovec's promotion he would soon learn of the London mole from the Director. Fortunately for his own sake, Klinovec was temporarily dormant in Moscow. Were he to re-establish contact with London, Moscow's man would realise that Klinovec was a traitor.

Hinkley didn't want Pilar calling. He telephoned her. He told her he'd be out of town for a week. He'd be leaving immediately. He would contact her when he got back.

'I don't care,' she said scornfully.

Bless you, thought Hinkley.

He stuffed a pair of trousers and socks with other articles of clothing; he put shoes on the socks; he laid the dummy legs behind the couch so that they protruded when viewed from the door.

To ensure that he was not observed through the balcony window, he crouched in the corner of the room where the outer wall met the wall in which the door was set. It was only three paces to the door from that corner, but he would have to move quickly if he was to surprise the caller with the flex he had pulled from the standard lamp. He was relying on the caller to step far enough into the room to allow him to attack from behind.

It would be a stranger watching the apartment: perhaps the old man he had observed loitering, the one whose teeth were too big for his mouth because his mouth had shrunk. Hinkley was sure there would be a caller. Someone would come to make sure he was dead. A casual caller. A 'friend'. They might even telephone the police, say they had looked through the letterbox when they had got no reply, and had seen Jack lying on the floor.

Hinkley would stay crouched in his apartment. He would do what they were doing outside, what they had all been trained to do: he would wait and see.

4

The Barcelona newspapers carried the story on the lower half of the front page. SECOND BRITISH DIPLOMAT FOUND MURDERED.

For Jack Hinkley, the waiting had ended. His body had been lying in his apartment for about twelve hours before it was discovered by Pilar. She had called to feed the cat. Hinkley had been shot. Shot at close range. This time the gunman had made sure he didn't miss.

There was dismay at the news in Century House. It was a Sunday afternoon when the message came from Barcelona. The news reached Pickering at his home. He sent for Lockwood, but was told that Lockwood had taken a weekend break in Paris. Lockwood would personally take charge of the inquiry on his return the following morning.